MARY POPPINS

From the moment when Mary Poppins, blown in by the East Wind, unpacked her carpet-bag in the nursery of Number 17 Cherry Tree Lane, Jane and Michael knew that no ordinary nurse had come to look after them. 'I'll stay till the wind changes,' she said. And so she did.

But before the wind changed, Mary Poppins took Jane and Michael to tea on the ceiling with her uncle, and to buy gingerbread from an old lady whose fingers were made of barley sugar. Her medicine changed flavour and tasted delicious to each of them and she rewarded good behaviour with magic.

Not surprisingly, when the wind did change and she flew off with her parrot-headed umbrella Jane and Michael and the twins were as desolate as you will be.

Mary Poppins will be particularly enjoyed by children from seven to eleven.

MARY POPPINS

P. L. Travers

with illustrations by
Mary Shepard

COLLINS
ARMADA LIONS

First published 1934 by Peter Davies
First published in Armada Lions 1971
by William Collins Sons and Co Ltd
14 St James's Place, London SW1
Second Impression July 1971
Third Impression December 1971

© P. L. Travers 1934

Printed in Great Britain by
William Collins Sons and Co Ltd, Glasgow

To
My Mother
1875–1928

Contents

CHAPTER I

East Wind

If you want to find Cherry Tree Lane all you have to do is ask the Policeman at the cross-roads. He will push his helmet slightly to one side, scratch his head thoughtfully, and then he will point his huge white-gloved finger and say: 'First to your right, second to your left, sharp right again, and you're there. Good-morning.'

And sure enough, if you follow his directions exactly, you *will* be there – right in the middle of Cherry Tree Lane, where the houses run down one side and the Park runs down the other and the cherry trees go dancing right down the middle.

If you are looking for Number Seventeen – and it is more than likely that you will be, for this book is all about that particular house – you will very soon find it. To begin with, it is the smallest house in the Lane. And besides that, it is the only one that is rather dilapidated and needs a coat of paint. But Mr Banks, who owns it, said to Mrs Banks that she could have either a nice, clean, comfortable house or four children. But not both, for he couldn't afford it.

And after Mrs Banks had given the matter some consideration she came to the conclusion that she would rather have Jane, who was the eldest, and Michael, who came next, and John and Barbara, who were twins and came last of all. So it was settled, and that was how the Banks family came to live at Number Seventeen, with Mrs Brill to cook for them, and Ellen to lay the tables, and Robertson Ay to cut the lawn and clean the knives and polish the shoes and, as Mr Banks always said, 'to waste his time and my money.'

And, of course, besides these there was Katie Nanna, who doesn't really deserve to come into the book at all because, at the time I am speaking of, she had just left Number Seventeen.

'Without by your leave or a word of warning. And what am I to do?' said Mrs Banks.

'Advertise, my dear,' said Mr Banks, putting on his shoes. 'And I wish Robertson Ay would go without a word of warning, for he has again polished one boot and left the other untouched. I shall look very lopsided.'

'That,' said Mrs Banks, 'is not of the least importance. You haven't told me what I'm to do about Katie Nanna.'

'I don't see how you can do anything about her since she has disappeared,' replied Mr Banks. 'But if it were me – I mean I – well, I should get somebody to put in the *Morning Paper* the news that Jane and Michael and John and Barbara Banks (to say nothing of their Mother) require the best possible Nannie at the lowest possible wage and at once. Then I should wait and watch for the Nannies to queue up outside the front gate, and I should get very cross with them for holding up the traffic and making it necessary for me to give the Policeman a shilling for putting him to so much trouble. Now I must be off.

Whew, it's as cold as the North Pole. Which way is the wind blowing?'

And as he said that, Mr Banks popped his head out of the window and looked down the Lane to Admiral Boom's house at the corner. This was the grandest house in the Lane, and the Lane was very proud of it because it was built exactly like a ship. There was a flagstaff in the garden, and on the roof was a gilt weathercock shaped like a telescope.

'Ha!' said Mr Banks, drawing in his head very quickly. 'Admiral's telescope says East Wind. I thought as much. There is frost in my bones. I shall wear two overcoats.' And he kissed his wife absentmindedly on one side of her nose and waved to the children and went away to the City.

Now, the City was a place where Mr Banks went every day – except Sundays, of course, and Bank Holidays – and while he was there he sat on a large chair in front of a large desk and made money. All day long he worked, cutting out pennies and shillings and half-crowns and threepenny-bits. And he brought them home with him in his little black bag. Sometimes he would give some to Jane and Michael for their money-boxes, and when he couldn't spare any he would say, 'The Bank is broken,' and they would know he hadn't made much money that day.

Well, Mr Banks went off with his black bag, and Mrs Banks went into the drawing-room and sat there all day long writing letters to the papers and begging them to send some Nannies to her at once as she was waiting; and

upstairs in the Nursery, Jane and Michael watched at the window and wondered who would come. They were glad Katie Nanna had gone, for they had never liked her. She was old and fat and smelt of barley-water. Anything, they thought, would be better than Katie Nanna – if not *much* better.

When the afternoon began to die away behind the Park, Mrs Brill and Ellen came to give them their supper and to bath the Twins. And after supper Jane and Michael sat at the window watching for Mr Banks to come home, and listening to the sound of the East Wind blowing through the naked branches of the cherry trees in the Lane. The trees themselves, turning and bending in the half light, looked as though they had gone mad and were dancing their roots out of the ground.

'There he is!' said Michael, pointing suddenly to a shape that banged heavily against the gate. Jane peered through the gathering darkness.

'That's not Daddy,' she said. 'It's somebody else.'

Then the shape, tossed and bent under the wind, lifted the latch of the gate, and they could see that it belonged to a woman, who was holding her hat on with one hand and carrying a bag in the other. As they watched, Jane and Michael saw a curious thing happen. As soon as the shape was inside the gate the wind seemed to catch her up into the air and fling her at the house. It was as though it had flung her first at the gate, waited for her to open it, and then lifted and thrown her, bag and all, at the front door. The watching children heard a terrific bang, and as she landed the whole house shook.

'How funny! I've never seen that happen before,' said Michael.

'Let's go and see who it is!' said Jane, and taking Michael's arm she drew him away from the window, through the Nursery and out on to the landing. From there they always had a good view of anything that happened in the front hall.

Presently they saw their Mother coming out of the drawing-room with a visitor following her. Jane and Michael could see that the newcomer had shiny black hair – 'Rather like a wooden Dutch doll,' whispered Jane.

And that she was thin, with large feet and hands, and small, rather peering blue eyes.

'You'll find that they are very nice children,' Mrs Banks was saying.

Michael's elbow gave a sharp dig at Jane's ribs.

'And that they give no trouble at all,' continued Mrs Banks uncertainly, as if she herself didn't really believe what she was saying. They heard the visitor sniff as though *she* didn't either.

'Now, about references – ' Mrs Banks went on.

'Oh, I make it a rule never to give references,' said the other firmly. Mrs Banks stared.

'But I thought it was usual,' she said. 'I mean – I understood people always did.'

'A very old-fashioned idea, to *my* mind,' Jane and Michael heard the stern voice say. '*Very* old-fashioned. *Quite* out of date, as you might say.'

Now, if there was one thing Mrs Banks did not like, it was to be thought old-fashioned. She just couldn't bear it. So she said quickly:

'Very well, then. We won't bother about them. I only asked, of course, in case *you* – er – required it. The nursery is upstairs – ' And she led the way towards the staircase, talking all the time, without stopping once. And because she was doing that Mrs Banks did not notice what was happening behind her, but Jane and Michael, watching from the top landing, had an excellent view of the extraordinary thing the visitor now did.

Certainly she followed Mrs Banks upstairs, but not in the usual way. With her large bag in her hands she slid

Holding her hat on with one hand and carrying
a bag in the other

gracefully *up* the banisters, and arrived at the landing at the same time as Mrs Banks. Such a thing, Jane and Michael knew, had never been done before. Down, of course, for they had often done it themselves. But up – never! They gazed curiously at the strange new visitor.

'Well, that's all settled, then.' A sigh of relief came from the children's Mother.

'Quite. As long as *I'm* satisfied,' said the other, wiping her nose with a large red and white bandanna handkerchief.

'Why, children,' said Mrs Banks, noticing them suddenly, 'what are you doing there? This is your new nurse, Mary Poppins. Jane, Michael, say how do you do! And these' – she waved her hand at the babies in their cots – 'are the Twins.'

Mary Poppins regarded them steadily, looking from one to the other as though she were making up her mind whether she liked them or not.

'Will we do?' said Michael.

'Michael, don't be naughty,' said his Mother.

Mary Poppins continued to regard the four children searchingly. Then, with a long, loud sniff that seemed to indicate that she had made up her mind, she said:

'I'll take the position.'

'For all the world,' as Mrs Banks said to her husband later, 'as though she were doing us a signal honour.'

'Perhaps she is,' said Mr Banks, putting his nose round the corner of the newspaper for a moment and then withdrawing it very quickly.

When their Mother had gone, Jane and Michael edged

towards Mary Poppins, who stood, still as a post, with her hands folded in front of her.

'How did you come?' Jane asked. 'It looked just as if the wind blew you here.'

'It did,' said Mary Poppins briefly. And she proceeded to unwind her muffler from her neck and to take off her hat, which she hung on one of the bed-posts.

As it did not seem as though Mary Poppins were going to say any more – though she sniffed a great deal – Jane, too, remained silent. But when she bent down to undo her bag, Michael could not restrain himself.

'What a funny bag!' he said, pinching it with his fingers.

'Carpet,' said Mary Poppins, putting her key in the lock.

'To carry carpets in, you mean?'

'No. Made of.'

'Oh,' said Michael. 'I see.' But he didn't – quite.

By this time the bag was open, and Jane and Michael were more than surprised to find it was completely empty.

'Why,' said Jane, 'there's nothing in it!'

'What do you mean – nothing?' demanded Mary Poppins, drawing herself up and looking as though she had been insulted. 'Nothing in it, did you say?'

And with that she took out from the empty bag a starched white apron and tied it round her waist. Next she unpacked a large cake of Sunlight Soap, a tooth-brush, a packet of hairpins, a bottle of scent, a small folding arm-chair and a box of throat lozenges.

Jane and Michael stared.

'But I *saw*,' whispered Michael. 'I'm sure it was empty.'

'Hush!' said Jane, as Mary Poppins took out a large bottle labelled 'One Tea-Spoon to be Taken at Bed-Time.'

A spoon was attached to the neck of the bottle, and into this Mary Poppins poured a dark crimson fluid.

'Is that your medicine?' inquired Michael, looking very interested.

'No, yours,' said Mary Poppins, holding out the spoon to him. Michael stared. He wrinkled up his nose. He began to protest.

'I don't want it. I don't need it. I won't!'

But Mary Poppins' eyes were fixed upon him, and Michael suddenly discovered that you could not look at Mary Poppins and disobey her. There was something strange and extraordinary about her – something that was frightening and at the same time most exciting. The spoon came nearer. He held his breath, shut his eyes and gulped. A delicious taste ran round his mouth. He turned his tongue in it. He swallowed, and a happy smile ran round his face.

'Strawberry ice,' he said ecstatically. 'More, more, more!'

But Mary Poppins, her face as stern as before, was pouring out a dose for Jane. It ran into the spoon, silvery, greeny, yellowy. Jane tasted it.

'Lime-juice cordial,' she said, sliding her tongue deliciously over her lips. But when she saw Mary Poppins moving towards the Twins with the bottle Jane rushed at her.

'Oh, no – please. They're too young. It wouldn't be good for them. Please!'

Mary Poppins, however, took no notice, but with a

warning, terrible glance at Jane, tipped the spoon towards
John's mouth. He lapped at it eagerly, and by the few drops
that were spilt on his bib, Jane and Michael could tell that
the substance in the spoon this time was milk. Then
Barbara had her share, and she gurgled and licked the
spoon twice.

Mary Poppins then poured out another dose and
solemnly took it herself.

'Rum punch,' she said, smacking her lips and corking
the bottle.

Jane's eyes and Michael's popped with astonishment,
but they were not given much time to wonder, for Mary
Poppins, having put the miraculous bottle on the mantelpiece, turned to them.

'Now,' she said, 'spit-spot into bed.' And she began to
undress them. They noticed that whereas buttons and
hooks had needed all sorts of coaxing from Katie Nanna,
for Mary Poppins they flew apart almost at a look. In less
than a minute they found themselves in bed and watching, by the dim light from the night-light, the rest of
Mary Poppins' unpacking being performed.

From the carpet-bag she took out seven flannel nightgowns, four cotton ones, a pair of boots, a set of dominoes,
two bathing-caps and a postcard album. Last of all came a
folding camp-bedstead with blankets and eiderdown com-
plete, and this she set down between John's cot and
Barbara's.

Jane and Michael sat hugging themselves and watching.
It was all so surprising that they could find nothing to say.
But they knew, both of them, that something strange and

wonderful had happened at Number Seventeen, Cherry Tree Lane.

Mary Poppins, slipping one of the flannel nightgowns over her head, began to undress underneath it as though it were a tent. Michael, charmed by this strange new arrival, unable to keep silent any longer, called to her.

'Mary Poppins,' he cried, 'you'll never leave us, will you?'

There was no reply from under the nightgown. Michael could not bear it.

'You won't leave us, will you?' he called anxiously.

Mary Poppins' head came out of the top of the nightgown. She looked very fierce.

'One word more from that direction,' she said threateningly, 'and I'll call the Policeman.'

'I was only saying,' began Michael, meekly, 'that we hoped you wouldn't be going away soon –' He stopped, feeling very red and confused.

Mary Poppins stared from him to Jane in silence. Then she sniffed.

'I'll stay till the wind changes,' she said shortly, and she blew out her candle and got into bed.

'That's all right,' said Michael, half to himself and half to Jane. But Jane wasn't listening. She was thinking about all that had happened, and wondering . . .

And that is how Mary Poppins came to live at Number Seventeen, Cherry Tree Lane. And although they sometimes found themselves wishing for the quieter, more

ordinary days when Katie Nanna ruled the household,
everybody, on the whole, was glad of Mary Poppins'
arrival. Mr Banks was glad because, as she arrived by herself and did not hold up the traffic, he had not had to tip
the Policeman. Mrs Banks was glad because she was able to
tell everybody that *her* children's nurse was so fashionable
that she didn't believe in giving references. Mrs Brill and
Ellen were glad because they could drink strong cups of
tea all day in the kitchen and no longer needed to preside
at nursery suppers. Robertson Ay was glad, too, because
Mary Poppins had only one pair of shoes, and those she
polished herself.

But nobody ever knew what Mary Poppins felt about it,
for Mary Poppins never told anybody anything . . .

CHAPTER 2

The Day Out

'Every third Thursday,' said Mrs Banks. 'Two till five.'

Mary Poppins eyed her sternly. 'The best people, ma'am,' she said, 'give every *second* Thursday, and one till six. And those I shall take or – ' Mary Poppins paused, and Mrs Banks knew what the pause meant. It meant that if she didn't get what she wanted Mary Poppins would not stay.

'Very well, very well,' said Mrs Banks hurriedly, though she wished Mary Poppins did not know so very much more about the best people than she did herself.

So Mary Poppins put on her white gloves and tucked her umbrella under her arm – not because it was raining but because it had such a beautiful handle that she couldn't possibly leave it at home. How could you leave your umbrella behind if it had a parrot's head for a handle? Besides, Mary Poppins was very vain and liked to look her best. Indeed, she was quite sure that she never looked anything else.

Jane waved to her from the Nursery window.

'Where are you going?' she called.

'Kindly close that window,' replied Mary Poppins, and Jane's head hurriedly disappeared inside the Nursery.

Mary Poppins walked down the garden-path and opened the gate. Once outside in the Lane, she set off walking very quickly as if she were afraid the afternoon would run away from her if she didn't keep up with it. At the corner she turned to the right and then to the left, nodded haughtily to the Policeman, who said it was a nice day, and by that time she felt that her Day Out had begun.

She stopped beside an empty motor-car in order to put her hat straight with the help of the windscreen, in which it was reflected, then she smoothed down her frock and tucked her umbrella more securely under her arm so that the handle, or rather the parrot, could be seen by every-body. After these preparations she went forward to meet the Match Man.

Now, the Match Man had two professions. He not only sold matches like any ordinary match man, but he drew pavement pictures as well. He did these things turn-about according to the weather. If it was wet, he sold matches because the rain would have washed away his pictures if he had painted them. If it was fine, he was on his knees all day, making pictures in coloured chalks on the side-walks, and doing them so quickly that often you would find he had painted up one side of a street and down the other almost before you'd had time to come round the corner.

On this particular day, which was fine but cold, he was painting. He was in the act of adding a picture of two Bananas, an Apple, and a head of Queen Elizabeth to a long string of others, when Mary Poppins walked up to him, tip-toeing so as to surprise him.

'Hey!' called Mary Poppins softly.

He went on putting brown stripes on a banana and brown curls on Queen Elizabeth's head.

'Ahem!' said Mary Poppins, with a ladylike cough.

He turned with a start and saw her.

'Mary!' he cried, and you could tell by the way he cried it that Mary Poppins was a very important person in his life.

Mary Poppins looked down at her feet and rubbed

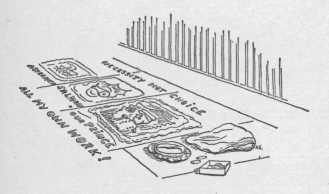

the toe of one shoe along the pavement two or three times. Then she smiled at the shoe in such a way that the shoe knew quite well that the smile wasn't meant for it.

'It's my Day, Bert,' she said. 'Didn't you remember?' Bert was the Match Man's name – Herbert Alfred for Sundays.

'Of course I remembered, Mary,' he said, 'but – ' and he stopped and looked sadly into his cap. It lay on the

ground beside his last picture and there was tuppence in
it. He picked it up and jingled the pennies.

'That all you got, Bert?' said Mary Poppins, and she said
it so brightly you could hardly tell she was disappointed
at all.

'That's the lot,' he said. 'Business is bad to-day. You'd
think anybody'd be glad to pay to see that, wouldn't
you?' And he nodded his head at Queen Elizabeth. 'Well –
that's how it is, Mary,' he sighed. 'Can't take you to tea to-
day, I'm afraid.'

Mary Poppins thought of the raspberry-jam-cakes they
always had on her Day Out, and she was just going to
sigh, when she saw the Match Man's face. So, very cleverly,
she turned the sigh into a smile – a good one with both
ends turned up – and said:

'That's all right, Bert. Don't you mind. I'd much rather
not go to tea. A stodgy meal, I call it – really.'

And that, when you think how very much she liked
raspberry-jam-cakes, was rather nice of Mary Poppins.

The Match Man apparently thought so, too, for he took
her white-gloved hand in his and squeezed it hard. Then
together they walked down the row of pictures.

'Now, *there's* one you've never seen before!' said the
Match Man proudly, pointing to a painting of a mountain
covered with snow and its slopes simply littered with
grasshoppers sitting on gigantic roses.

This time Mary Poppins could indulge in a sigh without
hurting his feelings.

'Oh, Bert,' she said, 'that's a fair treat!' And by the way
she said it she made him feel that by rights the picture

should have been in the Royal Academy, which is a large room where people hang the pictures they have painted. Everybody comes to see them, and when they have looked at them for a very long time, everybody says to everybody else: 'The idea – my dear!'

The next picture Mary Poppins and the Match Man came to was even better. It was the country – all trees and grass and a little bit of blue sea in the distance, and something that looked like Margate in the background.

'My word!' said Mary Poppins admiringly, stooping so that she could see it better. 'Why, Bert, whatever is the matter?'

For the Match Man had caught hold of her other hand now and was looking very excited.

'Mary,' he said, 'I got an idea! A real *idea*. Why don't we go there – right now – this very day? Both together, into the picture. Eh, Mary?' And still holding her hands he drew her right out of the street, away from the iron railings and the lamp-posts, into the very middle of the picture. Pff! There they were, right inside it!

How green it was there and how quiet, and what soft crisp grass under their feet! They could hardly believe it was true, and yet here were green branches huskily rattling on their hats as they bent beneath them, and little coloured flowers curling round their shoes. They stared at each other, and each noticed that the other had changed. To Mary Poppins, the Match Man seemed to have bought himself an entirely new suit of clothes, for he was now wearing a bright green-and-red striped coat and white flannel trousers and, best of all, a new straw hat. He looked unusually clean, as though he had been polished.

'Why, Bert, you look fine!' she cried in an admiring voice.

Bert could not say anything for a moment, for his mouth had fallen open and he was staring at her with round eyes. Then he gulped and said: 'Golly!'

That was all. But he said it in such a way and stared so steadily and so delightedly at her that she took a little mirror out of her bag and looked at herself in it.

She, too, she discovered, had changed. Round her shoulders hung a cloak of lovely artificial silk with watery patterns all over it, and the tickling feeling at the back of her neck came, the mirror told her, from a long curly feather that swept down from the brim of her hat. Her best shoes had disappeared, and in their place were others much finer and with large diamond buckles shining upon them. She was still wearing the white gloves and carrying the umbrella.

'My goodness,' said Mary Poppins, 'I *am* having a Day Out!'

So, still admiring themselves and each other, they moved on together through the little wood, till presently they came upon a little open space filled with sunlight. And there on a green table was Afternoon-Tea!

A pile of raspberry-jam-cakes as high as Mary Poppins' waist stood in the centre, and beside it tea was boiling in a big brass urn. Best of all, there were two plates of whelks and two pins to pick them out with.

'Strike me pink!' said Mary Poppins. That was what she always said when she was pleased.

'Golly!' said the Match Man. And that was *his* particular phrase.

'Won't you sit down, Moddom?' inquired a voice, and they turned to find a tall man in a black coat coming out of the wood with a table-napkin over his arm.

Mary Poppins, thoroughly surprised, sat down with a plop upon one of the little green chairs that stood round the table. The Match Man, staring, collapsed on to another.

'I'm the Waiter, you know!' explained the man in the black coat.

'Oh! But I didn't see you in the picture,' said Mary Poppins.

'Ah, I was behind the tree,' explained the Waiter.

'Won't you sit down?' asid Mary Poppins, politely.

'Waiters never sit down, Moddom,' said the man but he seemed pleased at being asked.

'Your whelks, Mister!' he said, pushing a plate of them over to the Match Man. '*And* your Pin!' He dusted the pin on his napkin and handed it to the Match Man.

They began upon the afternoon-tea, and the Waiter stood beside them to see they had everything they needed. 'We're having them after all,' said Mary Poppins in a loud whisper, as she began on the heap of raspberry-jam-cakes.

'Golly!' agreed the Match Man, helping himself to two of the largest.

'I'm the Waiter, you know!'

'Tea?' said the Waiter, filling a large cup for each of them from the urn.

They drank it and had two cups more each, and then, for luck, they finished the pile of raspberry-jam-cakes. After that they got up and brushed the crumbs off.

'There is Nothing to Pay,' said the Waiter, before they had time to ask for the bill. 'It is a Pleasure. You will find the Merry-go-Round just over there!' And he waved his hand to a little gap in the trees, where Mary Poppins and the Match Man could see several wooden horses whirling round on a stand.

'That's funny,' said she. 'I don't remember seeing that in the picture, either.'

'Ah,' said the Match Man, who hadn't remembered it himself, 'it was in the Background, you see!'

The Merry-go-Round was just slowing down as they approached it. They leapt upon it, Mary Poppins on a black horse and the Match Man on a grey. And when the music started again and they began to move, they rode all the way to Yarmouth and back, because that was the place they both wanted most to see.

When they returned it was nearly dark and the Waiter was watching for them.

'I'm very sorry, Moddom and Mister,' he said politely, 'but we close at Seven. Rules, you know. May I show you the Way Out?'

They nodded as he flourished his table-napkin and walked on in front of them through the wood.

'It's a wonderful picture you've drawn this time, Bert,'

said Mary Poppins, putting her hand through the Match
Man's arm and drawing her cloak about her.

'Well, I did my best, Mary,' said the Match Man mod-
estly. But you could see he was really very pleased with
himself indeed.

Just then the Waiter stopped in front of them, beside a
large white doorway that looked as though it were made
of thick chalk lines.

'Here you are!' he said. 'This is the Way Out.'

'Good-bye and thank you,' said Mary Poppins, shaking
his hand.

'Moddom, good-bye!' said the Waiter, bowing so low
that his head knocked against his knees.

He nodded to the Match Man, who cocked his head on
one side and closed one eye at the Waiter, which was his
way of bidding him farewell. Then Mary Poppins stepped
through the white doorway and the Match Man followed
her.

And as they went, the feather dropped from her hat and
the silk cloak from her shoulders and the diamonds from
her shoes. The bright clothes of the Match Man faded,
and his straw hat turned into his old ragged cap again.
Mary Poppins turned and looked at him, and she knew at
once what had happened. Standing on the pavement she
gazed at him for a long minute, and then her glance
explored the wood behind him for the Waiter. But the
Waiter was nowhere to be seen. There was nobody in the
picture. Nothing moved there. Even the Merry-go-Round
had disappeared. Only the still trees and the grass and the
unmoving little patch of sea remained.

But Mary Poppins and the Match Man smiled at one another. They knew, you see, what lay behind the trees . . .

When she came back from her Day Out, Jane and Michael came running to meet her.

'Where have you been?' they asked her.

'In Fairyland,' said Mary Poppins.

'Did you see Cinderella?' said Jane.

'Huh, Cinderella? Not me,' said Mary Poppins, contemptuously. 'Cinderella, indeed!'

'Or Robinson Crusoe?' asked Michael.

'Robinson Crusoe – pooh!' said Mary Poppins rudely.

'Then how could you have been there? It couldn't have been *our* Fairyland!'

Mary Poppins gave a superior sniff.

'Don't you know,' she said pityingly, 'that everybody's got a Fairyland of their own?'

And with another sniff she went upstairs to take off her white gloves and put the umbrella away.

CHAPTER 3

Laughing Gas

'Are you quite sure he will be at home?' said Jane, as they got off the Bus, she and Michael and Mary Poppins.

'Would my Uncle ask me to bring you to tea if he intended to go out, I'd like to know?' said Mary Poppins, who was evidently very offended by the question. She was wearing her blue coat with the silver buttons and the blue hat to match, and on the days when she wore these it was the easiest thing in the world to offend her.

All three of them were on the way to pay a visit to Mary Poppins' uncle, Mr Wigg, and Jane and Michael had looked forward to the trip for so long that they were more than half afraid that Mr Wigg might not be in, after all.

'Why is he called Mr Wigg – does he wear one?' asked Michael, hurrying along beside Mary Poppins.

'He is called Mr Wigg because Mr Wigg is his name. And he doesn't wear one. He is bald,' said Mary Poppins. 'And if I have any more questions we will just go Back Home.' And she sniffed her usual sniff of displeasure.

Jane and Michael looked at each other and frowned. And the frown meant: 'Don't let's ask her anything else or we'll never get there.'

Mary Poppins put her hat straight at the Tobacconist's Shop at the corner. It had one of those curious windows where there seem to be three of you instead of one, so that if you look long enough at them you begin to feel you are not yourself but a whole crowd of somebody else. Mary Poppins sighed with pleasure, however, when she saw three of herself, each wearing a blue coat with silver buttons and a blue hat to match. She thought it was such a lovely sight that she wished there had been a dozen of her or even thirty. The more Mary Poppins the better.

'Come along,' she said sternly, as though they had kept *her* waiting. Then they turned the corner and pulled the bell of Number Three, Robertson Road. Jane and Michael could hear it faintly echoing from a long way away and they knew that in one minute, or two at the most, they would be having tea with Mary Poppins' uncle, Mr Wigg, for the first time ever.

'If he's in, of course,' Jane said to Michael in a whisper.

At that moment the door flew open and a thin, watery-looking lady appeared.

'Is he in?' said Michael quickly.

'I'll thank you,' said Mary Poppins, giving him a terrible glance, 'to let *me* do the talking.'

'How do you do, Mrs Wigg,' said Jane politely.

'Mrs Wigg!' said the thin lady, in a voice even thinner than herself. 'How dare you call me Mrs Wigg? No, thank you! I'm plain Miss Persimmon *and* proud of it. Mrs Wigg indeed!' She seemed to be quite upset, and they thought Mr Wigg must be a very odd person if Miss Persimmon was so glad not to be Mrs Wigg.

'Straight up and first door on the landing,' said Miss

Persimmon, and she went hurrying away down the passage saying: 'Mrs Wigg indeed!' to herself in a high, thin, outraged voice.

Jane and Michael followed Mary Poppins upstairs. Mary Poppins knocked at the door.

'Come in! Come in! And welcome!' called a loud, cheery voice from inside. Jane's heart was pitter-pattering with excitement.

'He *is* in!' she signalled to Michael with a look.

Mary Poppins opened the door and pushed them in front of her. A large cheerful room lay before them. At one end of it a fire was burning brightly and in the centre stood an enormous table laid for tea – four cups and saucers, piles of bread and butter, crumpets, coconut cakes and a large plum cake with pink icing.

'Well, this is indeed a Pleasure,' a huge voice greeted them, and Jane and Michael looked round for its owner. He was nowhere to be seen. The room appeared to be quite empty. Then they heard Mary Poppins saying crossly:

'Oh, Uncle Albert – not *again*? It's not your birthday, is it?'

And as she spoke she looked up at the ceiling. Jane and Michael looked up too and to their surprise saw a round, fat, bald man who was hanging in the air without holding on to anything. Indeed, he appeared to be *sitting* on the air, for his legs were crossed and he had just put down the newspaper which he had been reading when they came in.

'My dear,' said Mr Wigg, smiling down at the children,

and looking apologetically at Mary Poppins, 'I'm very sorry, but I'm afraid it *is* my birthday.'

'Tch, tch, tch!' said Mary Poppins.

'I only remembered last night and there was no time then to send you a postcard asking you to come another day. Very distressing, isn't it?' he said, looking down at Jane and Michael.

'I can see you're rather surprised,' said Mr Wigg. And, indeed, their mouths were so wide open with astonishment that Mr Wigg, if he had been a little smaller, might almost have fallen into one of them.

'I'd better explain, I think,' Mr Wigg went on calmly. 'You see, it's this way. I'm a cheerful sort of man and very disposed to laughter. You wouldn't believe, either of you, the number of things that strike me as being funny. I can laugh at pretty nearly everything, I can.'

And with that Mr Wigg began to bob up and down, shaking with laughter at the thought of his own cheerfulness.

'Uncle Albert!' said Mary Poppins, and Mr Wigg stopped laughing with a jerk.

'Oh, beg pardon, my dear. Where was I? Oh, yes. Well, the funny thing about me is – all right, Mary, I won't laugh if I can help it! – that whenever my birthday falls on a Friday, well, it's all up with me. Absolutely UP,' said Mr Wigg.

'But why – ?' began Jane.

'But how – ?' began Michael.

'Well, you see, if I laugh on that particular day I become so filled with Laughing Gas that I simply can't keep on the ground. Even if I smile it happens. The first funny thought, and I'm up like a balloon. And until I can think of something serious I can't get down again.' Mr Wigg began to chuckle at that, but he caught sight of Mary Poppins' face and stopped the chuckle, and continued:

'It's awkward, of course, but not unpleasant. Never happens to either of you, I suppose?'

Jane and Michael shook their heads.

'No, I thought not. It seems to be my own special habit. Once, after I'd been to the Circus the night before, I laughed so much that – would you believe it? – I was up here for a whole twelve hours, and couldn't get down till the last stroke of midnight. Then, of course, I came down with a flop because it was Saturday and not my birthday any more. It's rather odd, isn't it? Not to say funny?

'And now here it is Friday again and my birthday, and you two and Mary P. to visit me. Oh, Lordy, Lordy, don't make me laugh, I beg of you – ' But although Jane and Michael had done nothing very amusing, except to stare at him in astonishment, Mr Wigg began to laugh again loudly, and as he laughed he went bouncing and bobbing about in the air, with the newspaper rattling in his hand and his spectacles half on and half off his nose.

He looked so comic, floundering in the air like a great human bubble, clutching at the ceiling sometimes and sometimes at the gas-bracket as he passed it, that Jane and Michael, though they were trying hard to be polite, just couldn't help doing what they did. They laughed. *And* they laughed. They shut their mouths tight to prevent the laughter escaping, but that didn't do any good. And presently they were rolling over and over on the floor, squealing and shrieking with laughter.

'Really!' said Mary Poppins. 'Really, *such* behaviour!'

'I can't help it, I can't help it!' shrieked Michael, as he rolled into the fender. 'It's so terribly funny. Oh, Jane, *isn't* it funny?'

Jane did not reply, for a curious thing was happening to her. As she laughed she felt herself growing lighter and lighter, just as though she were being pumped full of air. It was a curious and delicious feeling and it made her want to laugh all the more. And then suddenly, with a bouncing bound, she felt herself jumping through the air. Michael, to his astonishment, saw her go soaring up through the room. With a little bump her head touched the ceiling and then she went bouncing along it till she reached Mr Wigg.

'*Well!*' said Mr Wigg, looking very surprised indeed. 'Don't tell me it's *your* birthday, too?' Jane shook her head.

'It's not? Then this Laughing Gas must be catching! Hi – whoa there, look out for the mantelpiece!' This was to Michael, who had suddenly risen from the floor and was swooping through the air, roaring with laughter, and just grazing the china ornaments on the mantelpiece as he passed. He landed with a bounce right on Mr Wigg's knee.

'How do you do,' said Mr Wigg, heartily shaking Michael by the hand. 'I call this really friendly of you – bless my soul, I do! To come up to me since I couldn't come down to you – eh?' And then he and Michael looked at each other and flung back their heads and simply howled with laughter.

'I say,' said Mr Wigg to Jane, as he wiped his eyes. 'You'll be thinking I have the worst manners in the world. You're standing and you ought to be sitting – a nice young lady like you. I'm afraid I can't offer you a chair up here, but I think you'll find the air quite comfortable to sit on. I do.'

Jane tried it and found she could sit down quite comfortably on the air. She took off her hat and laid it down beside her and it hung there in space without any support at all.

'That's right,' said Mr Wigg. Then he turned and looked down at Mary Poppins.

'Well, Mary, we're fixed. And now I can inquire about *you*, my dear. I must say, I am very glad to welcome you and my two young friends here to-day – why, Mary, you're frowning. I'm afraid you don't approve of – er – all this.'

He waved his hand at Jane and Michael, and said hurriedly:

'I apologise, Mary, my dear. But you know how it is with me. Still, I must say I never thought my two young friends here would catch it, really I didn't, Mary! I suppose I should have asked them for another day or tried to think of something sad or something – '

'Well, I must say,' said Mary Poppins primly, 'that I have never in my life seen such a sight. And at your age, Uhcle – '

'Mary Poppins, Mary Poppins, do come up!' interrupted Michael. 'Think of something funny and you'll find it's quite easy.'

'Ah, now do, Mary!' said Mr Wigg persuasively.

'We're lonely up here without you!' said Jane, and held out her arms towards Mary Poppins. '*Do* think of something funny!'

'Ah, *she* doesn't need to,' said Mr Wigg sighing. 'She can come up if she wants to, even without laughing – and she knows it.' And he looked mysteriously and secretly at Mary Poppins as she stood down there on the hearth-rug.

'Well,' said Mary Poppins, 'it's all very silly and undignified, but, since you're all up there and don't seem able to get down, I suppose I'd better come up, too.'

With that, to the surprise of Jane and Michael, she put her hands down at her sides and without a laugh, without even the faintest glimmer of a smile, she shot up through the air and sat down beside Jane.

'How many times, I should like to know,' she said snappily, 'have I told you to take off your coat when you come into a hot room?' And she unbuttoned Jane's coat and laid it neatly on the air beside the hat.

'That's right, Mary, that's right,' said Mr Wigg contentedly, as he leant down and put his spectacles on the mantelpiece. 'Now we're all comfortable – '

'There's comfort *and* comfort,' sniffed Mary Poppins.

'And we can have tea,' Mr Wigg went on, apparently not noticing her remark. And then a startled look came over his face.

'My goodness!' he said. 'How dreadful! I've just realised – the table's down there and we're up here. What *are* we going to do? We're here and it's there. It's an awful tragedy – awful! But oh, it's terribly comic!' And he hid his face in his handkerchief and laughed loudly into it. Jane and Michael, though they did not want to miss the crumpets and the cakes, couldn't help laughing too, because Mr Wigg's mirth was so infectious.

Mr Wigg dried his eyes.

'There's only one thing for it,' he said. 'We must think of something serious. Something sad, very sad. And then we shall be able to get down. Now – one, two, three! Something *very* sad, mind you!'

They thought and thought, with their chins on their hands.

Michael thought of school, and that one day he would have to go there. But even that seemed funny to-day and he had to laugh.

Jane thought: 'I shall be grown up in another fourteen years!' But that didn't sound sad at all but quite nice and rather funny. She could not help smiling at the thought of herself grown up, with long skirts and a hand-bag.

'There was my poor old Aunt Emily,' thought Mr Wigg out loud. 'She was run over by an omnibus. Sad. Very sad. Unbearably sad. Poor Aunt Emily. But they saved her umbrella. That was funny, wasn't it?' And before he knew where he was, he was heaving and trembling and bursting with laughter at the thought of Aunt Emily's umbrella.

'It's no good,' he said, blowing his nose. 'I give it up And my young friends here seem to be no better at sadness

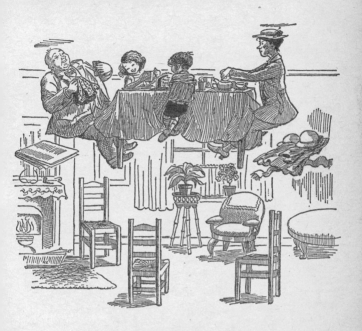

There they were, all together, up in the air

than I am. Mary, can't *you* do something? We want our tea.'

To this day Jane and Michael cannot be sure of what happened then. All they know for certain is that, as soon as Mr Wigg had appealed to Mary Poppins, the table below began to wriggle on its legs. Presently it was swaying dangerously, and then with a rattle of china and with cakes lurching off their plates on to the cloth, the table came soaring through the room, gave one graceful turn, and landed beside them so that Mr Wigg was at its head.

'Good girl!' said Mr Wigg, smiling proudly upon her. 'I knew you'd fix something. Now, will you take the foot of the table and pour out, Mary? And the guests on either side of me. That's the idea,' he said, as Michael ran bobbing through the air and sat down on Mr Wigg's right. Jane was at his left hand. There they were, all together, up in the air and the table between them. Not a single piece of bread-and-butter or a lump of sugar had been left behind.

Mr Wigg smiled contentedly.

'It is usual, I think, to begin with bread-and-butter,' he said to Jane and Michael, 'but as it's my birthday we will begin the wrong way – which I always think is the *right* way – with the Cake!'

And he cut a large slice for everybody.

'More tea?' he said to Jane. But before she had time to reply there was a quick, sharp knock at the door.

'Come in!' called Mr Wigg.

The door opened and there stood Miss Persimmon, with a jug of hot water on a tray.

'I thought, Mr Wigg,' she began, looking searchingly round the room, 'you'd be wanting some more hot – Well, I never! I simply *never*!' she said, as she caught sight of them all seated on the air round the table. 'Such goings on I never did see! In all my born days I never saw such. I'm sure, Mr Wigg, I always knew *you* were a bit odd. But I've closed my eyes to it – being as how you paid your rent regular. But such behaviour as this – having tea in the air with your guests – Mr Wigg, sir, I'm astonished at you! It's that undignified, and for a gentleman of your age – I never did – '

'But perhaps you will, Miss Persimmon!' said Michael.

'Will what?' said Miss Persimmon haughtily.

'Catch the Laughing Gas, as we did,' said Michael.

Miss Persimmon flung back her head scornfully.

'I hope, young man,' she retorted, 'I have more respect for myself than to go bouncing about in the air like a rubber ball on the end of a bat. I'll stay on my own feet, thank you, or my name's not Amy Persimmon, and – oh dear, oh *dear*, my goodness, oh *DEAR* – what *is* the matter? I can't walk, I'm going, I – oh, help, *HELP*!'

For Miss Persimmon, quite against her will, was off the ground and was stumbling through the air, rolling from side to side like a very thin barrel, balancing the tray in her hand. She was almost weeping with distress as she arrived at the table and put down her jug of hot water.

'Thank you,' said Mary Poppins in a calm, very polite voice.

Then Miss Persimmon turned and went wafting down again, murmuring as she went: 'So undignified – and me a well-behaved, steady-going woman. I must see a doctor – '

When she touched the floor she ran hurriedly out of the room, wringing her hands, and not giving a single glance backwards.

'So undignified!' they heard her moaning as she shut the door behind her.

'Her name can't be Amy Persimmon, because she *didn't* stay on her own feet!' whispered Jane to Michael.

But Mr Wigg was looking at Mary Poppins – a curious look, half-amusing, half-accusing.

'Mary, Mary, you shouldn't – bless my soul, you shouldn't, Mary. The poor old body will never get over it.

But, oh, my goodness, didn't she look funny waddling through the air – my Gracious Goodness, but didn't she?'

And he and Jane and Michael were off again, rolling about the air, clutching their sides and gasping with laughter at the thought of how funny Miss Persimmon had looked.

'Oh dear!' said Michael. 'Don't make me laugh any more. I can't stand it. I shall break!' 'Oh, oh, oh!' cried Jane, as she gasped for breath, with her hand over her heart. 'Oh, my Gracious, Glorious, Galumphing Goodness!' roared Mr Wigg, dabbing his eyes with his coat-tail because he couldn't find his handkerchief.

'IT IS TIME TO GO HOME.' Mary Poppins' voice sounded above the roars of laughter like a trumpet.

And suddenly, with a rush, Jane and Michael and Mr Wigg came down. They landed on the floor with a huge bump, all together. The thought that they would have to go home was the first sad thought of the afternoon, and the moment it was in their minds the Laughing Gas went out of them.

Jane and Michael sighed as they watched Mary Poppins come slowly down the air, carrying Jane's coat and hat.

Mr Wigg sighed, too. A great, long, heavy sigh.

'Well, isn't that a pity?' he said soberly. 'It's very sad that you've got to go home. I never enjoyed an afternoon so much – did you?'

'Never,' said Michael sadly, feeling how dull it was to be down on the earth again with no Laughing Gas inside him.

'Never, never,' said Jane, as she stood on tip-toe and

kissed Mr Wigg's withered-apple cheeks. 'Never, never, never, never . . .!'

They sat on either side of Mary Poppins going home in the Bus. They were both very quiet, thinking over the lovely afternoon. Presently Michael said sleepily to Mary Poppins:

'How often does your Uncle get like that?'

'Like what?' said Mary Poppins sharply, as though Michael had deliberately said something to offend her.

'Well – all bouncy and boundy and laughing and going up in the air.'

'Up in the air?' Mary Poppins' voice was high and angry. 'What do you mean, pray, up in the air?'

Jane tried to explain.

'Michael means – is your Uncle often full of Laughing Gas, and does he often go rolling and bobbing about on the ceiling when – '

'Rolling and bobbing! What an idea! Rolling and bobbing on the ceiling! You'll be telling me next he's a balloon!' Mary Poppins gave an offended sniff.

'But he did!' said Michael. 'We saw him.'

'What, roll and bob? How dare you! I'll have you know that my Uncle is a sober, honest, hard-working man, and you'll be kind enough to speak of him respectfully. And don't bite your Bus ticket! Roll and bob, indeed – the idea!'

Michael and Jane looked across Mary Poppins at each other. They said nothing, for they had learnt that it was

Crept closer to her and fell asleep

better not to argue with Mary Poppins, no matter how odd anything seemed.

But the look that passed between them said: 'Is it true or isn't it? About Mr Wigg. Is Mary Poppins right or are we?'

But there was nobody to give them the right answer.

The Bus roared on, wildly lurching and bounding.

Mary Poppins sat between them, offended and silent, and presently, because they were very tired, they crept closer to her and leant up against her sides and fell asleep, still wondering . . .

CHAPTER 4

Miss Lark's Andrew

Miss Lark lived Next Door.

But before we go any farther I must tell you what Next Door looked like. It was a very grand house, by far the grandest in Cherry Tree Lane. Even Admiral Boom had been known to envy Miss Lark her wonderful house, though his own had ship's funnels instead of chimneys and a flagstaff in the front garden. Over and over again the inhabitants of the Lane heard him say, as he rolled past Miss Lark's mansion: 'Blast my gizzard! What does *she* want with a house like that?'

And the reason of Admiral Boom's jealousy was that Miss Lark had two gates. One was for Miss Lark's friends and relations, and the other for the Butcher and the Baker and the Milkman.

Once the Baker made a mistake and came in through the gate reserved for the friends and relations, and Miss Lark was so angry that she said she wouldn't have any more bread ever.

But in the end she had to forgive the Baker because he was the only one in the neighbourhood who made those little flat rolls with the curly twists of crust on the top. She never really liked him very much after that, however, and when he came he pulled his hat far down over his eyes so that Miss Lark might think he was somebody else. But she never did.

Jane and Michael always knew when Miss Lark was in the garden or coming along the Lane, because she wore so many brooches and necklaces and earrings that she jingled and jangled just like a brass band. And whenever she met them, she always said the same thing:

'Good-morning!' (or 'Good-afternoon!' if it happened to be after luncheon), 'and how are *we* to-day?'

And Jane and Michael were never quite sure whether Miss Lark was asking how *they* were, or how she and Andrew were.

So they just replied: 'Good-afternoon!' (or, of course, 'Good-morning!' if it was before luncheon).

All day long, no matter where the children were, they could hear Miss Lark calling, in a very loud voice, things like:

'Andrew, where are you?' or

'Andrew, you mustn't go out without your overcoat!' or

'Andrew, come to Mother!'

And, if you didn't know, you would think that Andrew must be a little boy. Indeed, Jane thought that Miss Lark thought that Andrew *was* a little boy. But Andrew wasn't. He was a dog – one of those small, silky-fluffy dogs that look like a fur necklet, until they begin to bark. But, of course, when they do that you *know* that they're dogs. No fur necklet ever made a noise like that.

Now, Andrew led such a luxurious life that you might have thought he was the Shah of Persia in disguise. He slept on a silk pillow in Miss Lark's room; he went by car to the Hairdresser's twice a week to be shampooed; he had cream for every meal and sometimes oysters, and he possessed four overcoats with checks and stripes in different colours. Andrew's ordinary days were filled with the kind of things most people have only on birthdays. And when Andrew himself had a birthday he had *two* candles on his cake for every year, instead of only one.

The effect of all this was to make Andrew very much disliked in the neighbourhood. People used to laugh

heartily when they saw Andrew sitting up in the back seat of Miss Lark's car on the way to the Hairdresser's, with the fur rug over his knees and his best coat on. And on the day when Miss Lark bought him two pairs of small leather boots so that he could go out in the Park wet or fine, everybody in the Lane came down to their front gates to watch him go by and to smile secretly behind their hands.

'Pooh!' said Michael, as they were watching Andrew one day through the fence that separated Number Seventeen from Next Door. 'Pooh, he's a ninkypoop!'

'How do you know?' asked Jane, very interested.

'I know because I heard Daddy call him one this morning!' said Michael, and he laughed at Andrew very rudely.

'He is *not* a nincompoop,' said Mary Poppins. 'And that is that.'

And Mary Poppins was right. Andrew wasn't a nincompoop, as you will very soon see.

You must not think he did not respect Miss Lark. He did. He was even fond of her in a mild sort of way. He couldn't help having a kindly feeling for somebody who had been so good to him ever since he was a puppy, even if she *did* kiss him rather too often. But there was no doubt about it that the life Andrew led bored him to distraction. He would have given half his fortune, if he had one, for a nice piece of raw, red meat, instead of the usual breast of chicken or scrambled eggs with asparagus.

For in his secret, innermost heart, Andrew longed to be a common dog. He never passed his pedigree (which hung on the wall in Miss Lark's drawing-room) without a shudder of shame. And many a time he wished he'd never had a father, nor a grandfather, nor a great-grandfather, if Miss Lark was going to make such a fuss of it.

It was this desire of his to *be* a common dog that made Andrew choose common dogs for his friends. And whenever he got the chance, he would run down to the front gate and sit there watching for them, so that he could exchange a few common remarks. But Miss Lark, when she discovered him, would be sure to call out:

'Andrew, Andrew, come in, my darling! Come away from those dreadful street arabs!'

And of course Andrew would *have* to come in, or Miss

Lark would shame him by coming out and *bringing* him in. And Andrew would blush and hurry up the steps so that his friends should not hear her calling him her Precious, her Joy, her Little Lump of Sugar.

Andrew's most special friend was more than common, he was a Byword. He was half an Airedale and half a Retriever and the worst half of both. Whenever there was a fight in the road he would be sure to be in the thick of it; he was always getting into trouble with the Postman or the Policeman, and there was nothing he loved better than sniffing about in drains or garbage tins. He was, in fact, the talk of the whole street, and more than one person had been heard to say thankfully that they were glad he was not *their* dog.

But Andrew loved him and was continually on the watch for him. Sometimes they had only time to exchange a sniff in the Park, but on luckier occasions – though these were very rare – they would have long talks at the gate. From his friend, Andrew heard all the town gossip, and you could see by the rude way in which the other dog laughed as he told it, that it wasn't very complimentary.

Then suddenly, Miss Lark's voice would be heard calling from a window, and the other dog would get up, loll out his tongue at Miss Lark, wink at Andrew and wander off, waving his hind-quarters as he went just to show that *he* didn't care.

Andrew, of course, was never allowed outside the gate unless he went with Miss Lark for a walk in the Park, or with one of the maids to have his toes manicured.

Imagine, then, the surprise of Jane and Michael when

they saw Andrew, all alone, careering past them through the Park, with his ears back and his tail up as though he were on the track of a tiger.

Mary Poppins pulled the perambulator up with a jerk, in case Andrew, in his wild flight, should upset it and the Twins. And Jane and Michael screamed at him as he passed.

'Hi, Andrew! Where's your overcoat?' cried Michael, trying to make a high, windy voice like Miss Lark's.

'Andrew, you naughty little boy!' said Jane, and her voice, because she was a girl, was much more like Miss Lark's.

But Andrew just looked at them both very haughtily and barked sharply in the direction of Mary Poppins.

'Yay-yap!' said Andrew several times very quickly.

'Let me see. I think it's the first on your right and second house on the left-hand side,' said Mary Poppins.

'Yap?' said Andrew.

'No – no garden. Only a back-yard. Gate's usually open.'

Andrew barked again.

'I'm not sure,' said Mary Poppins. 'But I should think so. Generally goes home at tea-time.'

Andrew flung back his head and set off again at a gallop.

Jane's eyes and Michael's were round as saucers with surprise.

'What was he saying?' they demanded breathlessly, both together.

'Just passing the time of day!' said Mary Poppins, and

shut her mouth tightly as though she did not intend any more words to escape from it. John and Barbara gurgled from their perambulator.

'He wasn't!' said Michael.

'He *couldn't* have been!' said Jane.

'Well, you know best, of course. *As* usual,' said Mary Poppins haughtily.

'He must have been asking you where somebody lived, I'm sure he must – ' Michael began.

'Well, if you know, why bother to ask me?' said Mary Poppins sniffing. '*I'm* no dictionary.'

'Oh, Michael,' said Jane, 'she'll never tell us if you talk like that. Mary Poppins, do say what Andrew was saying to you, *please*.'

'Ask *him*. He knows – Mr Know-All!' said Mary Poppins, nodding her head scornfully at Michael.

'Oh no, I don't. I promise I don't, Mary Poppins. Do tell.'

'Half-past three. Tea-time,' said Mary Poppins, and she wheeled the perambulator round and shut her mouth tight again as though it were a trap-door. She did not say another word all the way home.

Jane dropped behind with Michael.

'It's your fault!' she said. 'Now we'll never know.'

'I don't care!' said Michael, and he began to push his scooter very quickly. 'I don't want to know.'

But he did want to know very badly indeed. And as it turned out, he and Jane and everybody else knew all about it before tea-time.

Just as they were about to cross the road to their own

house, they heard loud cries coming from Next Door, and
there they saw a curious sight. Miss Lark's two maids were
rushing wildly about the garden, looking under bushes
and up into the trees as people do who have lost their
most valuable possession. And there was Robertson Ay,
from Number Seventeen, busily wasting his time by poking at the gravel on Miss Lark's path with a broom as
though he expected to find the missing treasure under a
pebble. Miss Lark herself was running about in her garden,
waving her arms and calling: 'Andrew, Andrew! Oh, he's
lost. My darling boy is lost! We must send for the Police. I
must see the Prime Minister. Andrew is lost! Oh dear! oh
dear!'

'Oh, poor Miss Lark!' said Jane, hurrying across the road.
She could not help feeling sorry because Miss Lark looked
so upset.

But it was Michael who really comforted Miss Lark.
Just as he was going in at the gate of Number Seventeen,
he looked down the Lane and there he saw –

'Why, there's Andrew, Miss Lark. See, down there – just
turning Admiral Boom's corner!'

'Where, where? Show me!' said Miss Lark breathlessly,
and she peered in the direction in which Michael was
pointing.

And there, sure enough, *was* Andrew, walking as slowly
and as casually as though nothing in the world was the
matter; and beside him waltzed a huge dog that seemed to
be half an Airedale and half a Retriever, and the worst half
of both.

Miss Lark was running about in her garden, calling:
'Andrew, Andrew! Oh, he's lost!'

'Oh, what a relief!' said Miss Lark, sighing loudly. 'What a load off my mind!'

Mary Poppins and the children waited in the Lane outside Miss Lark's gate. Miss Lark herself and her two maids leant over the fence, Robertson Ay, resting from his labours, propped himself up with his broom-handle, and all of them watched in silence the return of Andrew.

He and his friend marched sedately up to the group, whisking their tails jauntily and keeping their ears well cocked, and you could tell by the look in Andrew's eye that, whatever he meant, he meant business.

'That dreadful dog!' said Miss Lark, looking at Andrew's companion.

'Shoo! Shoo! Go home!' she cried.

But the dog just sat down on the pavement and scratched his right ear with his left leg and yawned.

'Go away! Go home! Shoo, I say!' said Miss Lark, waving her arms angrily at the dog.

'And you, Andrew,' she went on, 'come indoors this minute! Going out like that – all alone and without your overcoat. I am very displeased with you!'

Andrew barked lazily, but did not move.

'What do you mean, Andrew? Come in at once!' said Miss Lark.

Andrew barked again.

'He says,' put in Mary Poppins, 'that he's not coming in.'

Miss Lark turned and regarded her haughtily. 'How do *you* know what my dog says, may I ask? Of course he will come in.'

Andrew, however, merely shook his head and gave one or two low growls.

'He won't,' said Mary Poppins. 'Not unless his friend comes, too.'

'Stuff and nonsense,' said Miss Lark crossly. 'That *can't* be what he says. As if I could have a great hulking mongrel like that inside my gate.'

Andrew yapped three or four times.

'He says he means it,' said Mary Poppins. 'And what's more, he'll go and live with his friend unless his friend is allowed to come and live with him.'

'Oh, Andrew, you can't – you can't, really – after all I've done for you and everything!' Miss Lark was nearly weeping.

Andrew barked and turned away. The other dog got up.

'Oh, he *does* mean it!' cried Miss Lark. 'I see he does. He is going away.' She sobbed a moment into her handkerchief, then she blew her nose and said:

'Very well, then, Andrew. I give in. This – this common dog can stay. On condition, of course, that he sleeps in the coal-cellar.'

'He insists, ma'am, that that won't do. His friend must have a silk cushion just like his and sleep in your room too. Otherwise he will go and sleep in the coal-cellar with his friend,' said Mary Poppins.

'Andrew, how could you?' moaned Miss Lark. 'I shall never consent to such a thing.'

Andrew looked as though he were preparing to depart. So did the other dog.

'Oh, he's leaving me!' shrieked Miss Lark. 'Very well,

then, Andrew. It will be as you wish. He *shall* sleep in my room. But I shall never be the same again, never, never. Such a common dog!'

She wiped her streaming eyes and went on:

'I should never have thought it of you, Andrew. But I'll say no more, no matter what I think. And this – er – creature – I shall have to call Waif or Stray or –'

At that the other dog looked at Miss Lark very indignantly, and Andrew barked loudly.

'They say you must call him Willoughby and nothing else,' said Mary Poppins. 'Willoughby being his name.'

'Willoughby! What a name! Worse and worse!' said Miss Lark despairingly. 'What is he saying now?' For Andrew was barking again.

'He says that if he comes back you are never to make him wear overcoats or go to the Hairdresser's again – that's his last word,' said Mary Poppins.

There was a pause.

'Very well,' said Miss Lark at last. 'But I warn you, Andrew, if you catch your death of cold – don't blame me!'

And with that she turned and walked haughtily up the steps, sniffing away the last of her tears.

Andrew cocked his head towards Willoughby as if to say: 'Come on!' and the two of them waltzed side by side slowly up the garden path, waving their tails like banners, and followed Miss Lark into the house.

'He isn't a ninkypoop after all, you see,' said Jane, as they went upstairs to the nursery and Tea.

'No,' agreed Michael. 'But how do you think Mary Poppins knew?'

'I don't know,' said Jane. 'And she'll never, never tell us. I am sure of that . . .'

CHAPTER 5

The Dancing Cow

Jane, with her head tied up in Mary Poppins' bandanna handkerchief, was in bed with earache.

'What does it feel like?' Michael wanted to know.

'Like guns going off inside my head,' said Jane.

'Cannons?'

'No, pop-guns.'

'Oh,' said Michael. And he almost wished he could have earache, too. It sounded so exciting.

'Shall I tell you a story out of one of the books?' said Michael, going to the bookshelf.

'No. I just couldn't bear it,' said Jane, holding her ear with her hand.

'Well, shall I sit at the window and tell you what is happening outside?'

'Yes, do,' said Jane.

So Michael sat all the afternoon on the window-seat telling her everything that occurred in the Lane. And sometimes his accounts were very dull and sometimes very exciting.

'There's Admiral Boom!' he said once. 'He has come out of his gate and is hurrying down the Lane. Here he comes. His nose is redder than ever and he's wearing a top-hat. Now he is passing Next Door –'

'Is he saying "Blast my gizzard!"?' inquired Jane.

'I can't hear. I expect so. There's Miss Lark's second housemaid in Miss Lark's garden. And Robertson Ay is in *our* garden, sweeping up the leaves and looking at her over the fence. He is sitting down now, having a rest.'

'He has a weak heart,' said Jane.

'How do you know?'

'He told me. He said his doctor said he was to do as little as possible. And I heard Daddy say if Robertson Ay does what his doctor told him to he'll sack him. Oh, how it bangs and *bangs*!' said Jane, clutching her ear again.

'Hull*oh*!' said Michael excitedly from the window.

'What is it?' cried Jane, sitting up. 'Do tell me.'

'A very extraordinary thing. There's a cow down in the Lane,' said Michael, jumping up and down on the window-seat.

'A cow? A real cow – right in the middle of a town?

M.P.   C

How funny! Mary Poppins,' said Jane, 'there's a cow in the Lane, Michael says.'

'Yes, and it's walking very slowly, putting its head over every gate and looking round as though it had lost something.'

'I *wish* I could see it,' said Jane mournfully.

'Look!' said Michael, pointing downwards as Mary Poppins came to the window. 'A cow. Isn't that funny?'

Mary Poppins gave a quick, sharp glance down into the Lane. She started with surprise.

'Certainly not,' she said, turning to Jane and Michael. 'It's not funny at all. I know that cow. She was a great friend of my Mother's and I'll thank you to speak politely to her.' She smoothed her apron and looked at them both very severely.

'Have you known her long?' inquired Michael gently, hoping that if he was particularly polite he would hear something more about the cow.

'Since before she saw the King,' said Mary Poppins.

'And when was that?' asked Jane, in a soft encouraging voice.

Mary Poppins stared into space, her eyes fixed upon something that they could not see. Jane and Michael held their breath, waiting.

'It was long ago,' said Mary Poppins, in a brooding story-telling voice. She paused, as though she were remembering events that happened hundreds of years before that time. Then she went on dreamily, still gazing into the middle of the room, but without seeing anything.

The Red Cow – that's the name she went by. And very important and prosperous she was, too (so my Mother said). She lived in the best field in the whole district – a large one full of buttercups the size of saucers and dandelions standing up in it like soldiers. Every time she ate the head off one soldier, another grew up in its place, with a green military coat and a yellow busby.

She had lived there always – she often told my Mother that she couldn't remember the time when she hadn't lived in that field. Her world was bounded by green hedges and the sky and she knew nothing of what lay beyond these.

The Red Cow was very respectable, she always behaved like a perfect lady and she knew What was What. To her a thing was either black or white – there was nothing in between. Dandelions were either sweet or sour – there were never any moderately nice ones.

She led a very busy life. Her mornings were taken up in giving lessons to the Red Calf, her daughter, and in the afternoon she taught the little one deportment and mooing and all the things a really well brought up calf should know. Then they had their supper, and the Red Cow showed the Red Calf how to select a good blade of grass from a bad one; and when her child had gone to sleep at night she would go into a corner of the field and chew the cud and think her own quiet thoughts.

All her days were exactly the same. One Red Calf grew up and went away and another came in its place. And it was natural that the Red Cow should imagine that her life would always be the same as it had always been – indeed, she felt that she could ask for nothing better than for all her days to be alike till she came to the end of them.

But at the very moment she was thinking these thoughts, adventure, as she afterwards told my Mother, was stalking her. It came upon her one night when the stars themselves looked like dandelions in the sky and the moon a great daisy among the stars.

On this night, long after the Red Calf was asleep, the Red Cow stood up suddenly and began to dance. She danced wildly and beautifully and in perfect time, though she had no music to go by. Sometimes it was a polka, sometimes a Highland Fling and sometimes a special dance that she made up out of her own head. And in between these dances she would curtsey and make sweeping bows and knock her head against the dandelions.

'Dear me!' said the Red Cow to herself, as she began on a Sailor's Hornpipe. 'What an extraordinary thing! I always thought dancing improper, but it can't be since I myself am dancing. For I am a model cow.'

And she went on dancing, and thoroughly enjoying herself. At last, however, she grew tired and decided that she had danced enough and that she would go to sleep. But, to her great surprise, she found that she could not stop dancing. When she went to lie down beside the Red Calf, her legs would not let her. They went on capering and prancing and, of course, carrying her with them. Round and round the field she went, leaping and waltzing and stepping on tip-toe.

'Dear me!' she murmured at intervals with a lady-like accent. 'How very peculiar!' But she couldn't stop.

In the morning she was still dancing and the Red Calf had to take its breakfast of dandelions all by itself because the Red Cow could not remain still enough to eat.

All through the day she danced, up and down the meadow and round and round the meadow, with the Red Calf mooing piteously behind her. When the second night came, and she was still at it and still could not stop, she grew very worried. And at the end of a week of dancing she was nearly distracted.

'I must go and see the King about it,' she decided, shaking her head.

So she kissed her Red Calf and told it to be good. Then she turned and danced out of the meadow and went to tell the King.

She danced all the way, snatching little sprays of green food from the hedges as she went, and every eye that saw her stared with astonishment. But none of them were more astonished than the Red Cow herself.

At last she came to the Palace where the King lived. She pulled the bell-rope with her mouth, and when the gate opened she danced through it and up the broad garden path till she came to the flight of steps that led to the King's throne.

Upon this the King was sitting, busily making a new set of Laws. His Secretary was writing them down in a little red note-book, one after another, as the King thought of them. There were Courtiers and Ladies-in-Waiting everywhere, all very gorgeously dressed and all talking at once.

'How many have I made to-day?' asked the King, turning to the Secretary. The Secretary counted the Laws he had written down in the red note-book.

'Seventy-two, your Majesty,' he said, bowing low and taking care not to trip over his quill pen, which was a very large one.

'H'm. Not bad for an hour's work,' said the King, looking very pleased with himself. 'That's enough for to-day.' He stood up and arranged his ermine cloak very tastefully.

'Order my coach. I must go to the Barber's,' he said magnificently.

It was then that he noticed the Red Cow approaching. He sat down again and took up his sceptre.

'What have we here, ho?' he demanded, as the Red Cow danced to the foot of the steps.

'A Cow, your Majesty!' she answered simply.

'I can see *that*,' said the King. 'I still have my eyesight. But what do you want? Be quick, because I have an appointment with the Barber at ten. He won't wait for me longer than that and I *must* have my hair cut. And for goodness' sake stop jigging and jagging about like that!' he added irritably. 'It makes me quite giddy.'

'Quite giddy!' echoed all the Courtiers, staring.

'That's just my trouble, your Majesty. I *can't* stop!' said the Red Cow piteously.

'Can't stop? Nonsense!' said the King furiously. 'Stop at *once*! I, the King, command you!'

'Stop at once! The King commands you!' cried all the Courtiers.

The Red Cow made a great effort. She tried so hard to

'What have we here, ho?'

stop dancing that every muscle and every rib stood out like mountain ranges all over her. But it was no good. She just went on dancing at the foot of the King's steps.

'I *have* tried, your Majesty. And I can't. I've been dancing now for seven days running. And I've had no sleep. And very little to eat. A white-thorn spray or two – that's all. So I've come to ask your advice.'

'H'm – very curious,' said the King, pushing the crown on one side and scratching his head.

'Very curious,' said the Courtiers, scratching their heads, too.

'What does it feel like?' asked the King.

'Funny,' said the Red Cow. 'And yet,' she paused, as if choosing her words, 'it's rather a pleasant feeling, too. As if laughter were running up and down inside me.'

'*Extraordinary*,' said the King, and he put his chin on his hand and stared at the Red Cow, pondering on what was the best thing to do.

Suddenly he sprang to his feet and said:

'Good gracious!'

'What is it?' cried all the Courtiers.

'Why, don't you see?' said the King, getting very excited and dropping his sceptre. 'What an idiot I was not to have noticed it before. And what idiots *you* were!' he turned furiously upon the Courtiers. 'Don't you see that there's a fallen star caught on her horn?'

'So there is!' cried the Courtiers, as they all suddenly noticed the star for the first time. And as they looked it seemed to them that the star grew brighter.

'That's what's wrong!' said the King. 'Now, you Courtiers had better pull it off so that this – er – lady can stop dancing and have some breakfast. It's the star, madam, that is making you dance,' he said to the Red Cow. 'Now, come along, you!'

And he motioned to the Chief Courtier, who presented himself smartly before the Red Cow and began to tug at the star. It would not come off. The Chief Courtier was joined by one after another of the other Courtiers, until at last there was a long chain of them, each holding the man in front of him by the waist, and a tug-of-war began between the Courtiers and the star.

'Mind my head!' entreated the Red Cow.

'Pull harder!' roared the King.

They pulled harder. They pulled until their faces were red as raspberries. They pulled till they could pull no longer and all fell back, one on top of the other. The star did not move. It remained firmly fixed to the horn.

'Tch, tch, tch!' said the King. 'Secretary, look in the Encyclopædia and see what it says about cows with stars on their horns.'

The Secretary knelt down and began to crawl under the throne. Presently he emerged, carrying a large green book which was always kept there in case the King wanted to know anything.

He turned the pages.

'There's nothing at all, your Majesty, except the story of the Cow Who Jumped Over the Moon, and you know all about that.'

The King rubbed his chin, because that helped him to think.

He sighed irritably and looked at the Red Cow.

'All I can say,' he said, 'is that *you'd* better try that too.'

'Try what?' said the Red Cow.

'Jumping over the moon. It might have an effect. Worth trying, anyway.'

'Me?' said the Red Cow, with an outraged stare.

'Yes, you – who else?' said the King impatiently. He was anxious to get to the Barber's.

'Sire,' said the Red Cow, 'I beg you to remember that I am a decent respectable animal and have been taught from my infancy that jumping was no occupation for a lady.'

The King stood up and shook his sceptre at her.

'Madam,' he said, 'you came here for my advice and I have given it to you. Do you want to go on dancing for ever? Do you want to go hungry for ever? Do you want to go sleepless for ever?'

The Red Cow thought of the lush sweet taste of dandelions. She thought of meadow grass and how soft it was to lie on. She thought of her weary capering legs and how nice it would be to rest them. And she said to herself: 'Perhaps, just for once, it wouldn't matter and nobody – except the King – need know.'

'How high do you suppose it is?' she said aloud as she danced.

The King looked up at the Moon.

'At least a mile, I should think,' said he.

The Red Cow nodded. She thought so, too. For a moment she considered, and then she made up her mind.

'I never thought that I should come to this, your

Majesty. Jumping – and over the moon at that. But – I'll try it,' she said and curtseyed gracefully to the throne.

'Good,' said the King pleasantly, realising that he would be in time for the Barber, after all. 'Follow me!'

He led the way into the garden, and the Red Cow and the Courtiers followed him.

'Now,' said the King, when he reached the open lawn, 'when I blow the whistle – jump!'

He took a large golden whistle from his waistcoat pocket and blew into it lightly to make sure there was no dust in it.

The Red Cow danced at attention.

'Now – one!' said the King.

'Two!'

'Three!'

Then he blew the whistle.

The Red Cow, drawing in her breath, gave one huge tremendous jump and the earth fell away beneath her. She could see the figures of the King and the Courtiers growing smaller and smaller until they disappeared below. She herself shot upwards through the sky, with the stars spinning around her like great golden plates, and presently, in blinding light, she felt the cold rays of the moon upon her. She shut her eyes as she went over it, and as the dazzling gleam passed behind her and she bent her head towards the earth again, she felt the star slip down her horn. With a great rush it fell off and went rolling down the sky. And it seemed to her that as it disappeared into the darkness great chords of music came from it and echoed through the air.

In another minute the Red Cow had landed on the earth again. To her great surprise she found that she was not in the King's garden but in her own dandelion field.

And she had stopped dancing! Her feet were as steady as though they were made of stone and she walked as sedately as any other respectable cow. Quietly and serenely she moved across the field, beheading her golden soldiers as she went to greet the Red Calf.

'I'm so glad you're back!' said the Red Calf. 'I've been *so* lonely.' .

The Red Cow kissed it and fell to munching the meadow. It was her first good meal for a week. And by the time her hunger was satisfied she had eaten up several regiments. After that she felt better. She soon began to live her life just exactly as she had lived it before.

At first she enjoyed her quiet regular habits very much, and was glad to be able to eat her breakfast without dancing and to lie down in the grass and sleep at night instead of curtseying to the moon until the morning.

But after a little she began to feel uncomfortable and dissatisfied. Her dandelion field and her Red Calf were all very well, but she wanted something else and she couldn't think what it was. At last she realised that she was missing her star. She had grown so used to dancing and to the happy feeling the star had given her that she wanted to do a Sailor's Hornpipe and to have the star on her horn again.

She fretted, she lost her appetite, her temper was atrocious. And she frequently burst into tears for no reason at all. Eventually, she went to my Mother and told her the whole story and asked her advice.

'Good gracious, my dear!' my Mother said to her. 'You don't suppose that only one star ever fell out of the sky! Billions fall every night, I'm told. But they fall in different places, of course. You can't expect two stars to drop in the same field in one lifetime.'

'Then, you think – if I moved about a bit – ?' the Red Cow began, a happy, eager look coming into her eyes.

'If it were me,' said my Mother, 'I'd go and look for one.'

'I will,' said the Red Cow joyously. 'I will indeed.'

Mary Poppins paused.

'And that, I suppose, is why she was walking down Cherry Tree Lane,' Jane prompted gently.

'Yes,' whispered Michael, 'she was looking for her star.'

Mary Poppins sat up with a little start. The intent look had gone from her eyes and the stillness from her body.

'Come down from that window at once, sir!' she said crossly. 'I am going to turn on the lights.' And she hurried across the landing to the electric light switch.

'Michael!' said Jane in a careful whisper. 'Just have one look and see if the cow's still there.'

Hurriedly Michael peered through the gathering dusk.

'Quickly!' said Jane. 'Mary Poppins will be back in one minute. Can you see her?'

'No-o-o,' said Michael, staring out. 'Not a sign of her. She's gone.'

'I do hope she finds it!' said Jane, thinking of the Red

Cow roaming through the world looking for a star to stick on her horn.

'So do I,' said Michael as, at the sound of Mary Poppins' returning footsteps, he hurriedly pulled down the blind . . .

CHAPTER 6

Bad Tuesday

It was not very long afterwards that Michael woke up one morning with a curious feeling inside him. He knew, the moment he opened his eyes, that something was wrong but he was not quite sure what it was.

'What is to-day, Mary Poppins?' he inquired, pushing the bedclothes away from him.

'Tuesday,' said Mary Poppins. 'Go and turn on your bath. Hurry!' she said, as he made no effort to move. He turned over and pulled the bedclothes up over his head and the curious feeling increased.

'What did I say?' said Mary Poppins in that cold, clear voice that was always a Warning.

Michael knew now what was happening to him. He knew he was going to be naughty.

'I won't,' he said slowly, his voice muffled by the blanket.

Mary Poppins twitched the clothes from his hand and looked down upon him.

'I won't.'

He waited, wondering what she would do and was surprised when, without a word, she went into the bathroom and turned on the tap herself. He took his towel and went slowly in as she came out. And for the first time in his life Michael entirely bathed himself. He knew by this that he was in disgrace, and he purposely neglected to wash behind his ears.

'Shall I let out the water?' he inquired in the rudest voice he had.

There was no reply.

'Pooh, I don't care!' said Michael, and the hot heavy weight that was within him swelled and grew larger. 'I *don't* care!'

He dressed himself then, putting on his best clothes, that he knew were only for Sunday. And after that he went downstairs, kicking the banisters with his feet – a thing he knew he should not do as it waked up everybody else in the house. On the stairs he met Ellen, the house-maid, and as he passed her he knocked the hot-water jug out of her hand.

'Well, you *are* a clumsy,' said Ellen, as she bent down to mop up the water. 'That was for your father's shaving.'

'I meant to,' said Michael calmly.

Ellen's red face went quite white with surprise.

'*Meant* to? You *meant* – well, then, you're a very bad heathen boy, and I'll tell your Ma, so I will – '

'Do,' said Michael, and he went on down the stairs.

Well, that was the beginning of it. Throughout the rest of the day nothing went right with him. The hot, heavy feeling inside him made him do the most awful things, and as soon as he'd done them he felt extraordinarily pleased and glad and thought out some more at once.

In the kitchen Mrs Brill, the cook, was making scones.

'No, Master Michael,' she said, 'you *can't* scrape out the basin. It's not empty yet.'

And at that he let out his foot and kicked Mrs Brill very hard on the shin, so that she dropped the rolling-pin and screamed aloud.

'You kicked Mrs Brill? Kind Mrs Brill? I'm ashamed of you,' said his Mother a few minutes later when Mrs Brill had told her the whole story. 'You must beg her pardon at once. Say you're sorry, Michael!'

'But I'm not sorry. I'm glad. Her legs are too fat,' he said, and before they could catch him he ran away up the area steps and into the garden. There he purposely bumped into Robertson Ay, who was sound asleep on top of the best rock plants, and Robertson Ay was very angry.

'I'll tell your Pa!' he said threateningly.

'And I'll tell him you haven't cleaned the shoes this morning,' said Michael, and was a little astonished at himself. It was his habit and Jane's always to protect Robertson Ay, because they loved him and didn't want to lose him.

But he was not astonished for long, for he had begun to wonder what he could do next. And it was no time before he thought of something.

Through the bars of the fence he could see Miss Lark's Andrew daintily sniffing at the Next Door lawn and choosing for himself the best blades of grass. He called softly to Andrew and gave him a biscuit out of his own pocket, and while Andrew was munching it he tied Andrew's tail to the fence with a piece of string. Then he ran away with Miss Lark's angry, outraged voice screaming in his ears, and his body almost bursting with the exciting weight of that heavy thing inside him.

The door of his Father's study stood open – for Ellen had just been dusting the books. So Michael did a forbidden thing. He went in, sat down at his Father's desk, and with his Father's pen began to scribble on the blotter. Suddenly his elbow, knocking against the inkpot, upset it, and the chair and the desk and the quill pen and his own best clothes were covered with great spreading stains of blue ink. It looked dreadful, and fear of what would happen to him stirred within Michael. But, in spite of that, he didn't care – he didn't feel the least bit sorry.

'That child must be ill,' said Mrs Banks, when she was told by Ellen – who suddenly returned and discovered him – of the latest adventure. 'Michael, you shall have some syrup of figs.'

'I'm not ill. I'm weller than you,' said Michael rudely.

'Then you're simply naughty,' said his Mother. 'And you shall be punished.'

And, sure enough, five minutes later, Michael found himself standing in his stained clothes in a corner of the nursery, facing the wall.

Jane tried to speak to him when Mary Poppins was not looking, but he would not answer, and put out his tongue at her. When John and Barbara crawled along the floor and each took hold of one of his shoes and gurgled, he just pushed them roughly away. And all the time he was enjoying his badness, hugging it to him as though it were a friend, and not caring a bit.

'I *hate* being good,' he said aloud to himself, as he trailed after Mary Poppins and Jane and the perambulator on the afternoon walk to the Park.

'Don't dawdle,' said Mary Poppins, looking back at him.

But he went on dawdling and dragging the sides of his shoes along the pavement in order to scratch the leather.

Suddenly Mary Poppins turned and faced him, one hand on the handle of the perambulator.

'You,' she began, 'got out of bed the wrong side this morning.'

'I didn't,' said Michael. 'There is no wrong side to my bed.'

'Every bed has a right and a wrong side,' said Mary Poppins, primly.

'Not mine – it's next the wall.'

'That makes no difference. It's still a side,' scoffed Mary Poppins.

'Well, is the wrong side the left side or is the wrong side the right side? Because I got out on the right side, so how can it be wrong?'

'Both sides were the wrong side, this morning, Mr Smarty!'

'But it has only one, and if I got out the right side – ' he argued.

'One word more from you – ' began Mary Poppins, and she said it in such a peculiarly threatening voice that even Michael felt a little nervous. 'One more word and I'll – '

She did not say what she would do, but he quickened his pace.

'Pull yourself together, Michael,' said Jane in a whisper.

'You shut up,' he said, but so low that Mary Poppins could not hear.

'Now, sir,' said Mary Poppins. 'Off you go – in front of me, please. I'm not going to have you stravaiging behind any longer. You'll oblige me by going on ahead.' She pushed him in front of her. 'And,' she continued, 'there's a shiny thing sparkling on the path just along there. I'll thank you to go and pick it up and bring it to me. Somebody's dropped their tiara, perhaps.'

Against his will, but because he didn't dare not to, Michael looked in the direction in which she was pointing, Yes – there *was* something shining on the path. From that

distance it looked very interesting, and its sparkling rays of
light seemed to beckon him. He walked on, swaggering a
little, going as slowly as he dared and pretending that he
didn't really want to see what it was.

He reached the spot, and stooping, picked up the shining thing. It was a small round sort of box with a glass top
and on the glass an arrow marked. Inside, a round disc
that seemed to be covered with letters swung gently as he
moved the box.

Jane ran up and looked at it over his shoulder.

'What is it, Michael?' she asked.

'I won't tell you,' said Michael, though he didn't know
himself.

'Mary Poppins, what is it?' demanded Jane, as the perambulator drew up beside them. Mary Poppins took the little
box from Michael's hand.

'It's mine,' he said jealously.

'No, mine,' said Mary Poppins. 'I saw it first.'

'But I picked it up.' He tried to snatch it from her hand,
but she gave him such a look that his hand fell to his
side.

She tilted the round thing backwards and forwards,
and in the sunlight the disc and its letters went careering
madly inside the box.

'What's it for?' asked Jane.

'To go round the world with,' said Mary Poppins.

'Pooh!' said Michael. 'You go round the world in a ship,
or an aeroplane. *I* know that. The box thing wouldn't take
you round the world.'

'Oh, indeed – wouldn't it?' said Mary Poppins, with a

curious I-know-better-than-you expression on her face. 'You just watch!'

And holding the compass in her hand she turned towards the entrance of the Park and said the word 'North!'

The letters slid round the arrow, dancing giddily. Suddenly the atmosphere seemed to grow bitterly cold, and the wind became so icy that Jane and Michael shut their eyes against it. When they opened them the Park had entirely disappeared – not a tree nor a green-painted seat nor an asphalt footpath was in sight. Instead, they were surrounded by great boulders of blue ice and beneath their feet snow lay thickly frosted upon the ground.

'Oh, oh!' cried Jane, shivering with cold and surprise, and she rushed to cover the Twins with their perambulator rug. 'What *has* happened to us?'

Mary Poppins looked at Michael significantly. She had no time to reply, however, for at that moment, out of a hole in one of the boulders, an Eskimo man emerged, his round, brown face surrounded by a bonnet of white fur, and a long white fur coat over his shoulders.

'Welcome to the North Pole, Mary Poppins and Friends'! said the Eskimo, with a broad smile of welcome. Then he came forward and rubbed his nose against each of their noses in turn, as a sign of greeting. Presently a lady Eskimo came out of the hole carrying a baby Eskimo wrapped up in a sealskin shawl.

'Why, Mary, this *is* a treat!' she said, and she, too rubbed noses all round. 'You must be cold,' she said then, looking with surprise at their thin dresses. 'Let me get you some fur coats. We've just been skinning a couple of Polar

The compass

Bears. And you'd like some whale-blubber soup, wouldn't you, my dears?'

'I'm afraid we can't stay,' Mary Poppins rejoined quickly. 'We're going round the world, and only looked in for a moment, thank you all the same. Another time, perhaps.'

And, making a little movement of her hand, she spun the compass and said, 'South!'

It seemed to Jane and Michael then as if the whole world, like the compass, were spinning round and that they were in the middle of the spin, as one is when the conductor, as a special treat, takes you inside the works of a Merry-go-Round.

As the world swung round them they felt themselves getting warmer and warmer, and when it slowed down again and became steady they found themselves standing beside a grove of palm-trees. The sun spread a cloak of warmth around them and the sand was golden beneath their feet.

Under the palm-trees sat a man and a woman as black and shiny and plump as ripe plums, and wearing very few clothes. But to make up for this they wore a great many beads. Some hung round their foreheads below great crowns of feathers; others were looped about their ears; there were even one or two in their noses. They had necklaces of coloured beads and belts of plaited beads round their waists. And on the knee of the dark lady sat a tiny plum-black baby with nothing on at all! It smiled at the children as its Mother spoke.

'We've been anticipating your visit, Mary Poppins,' she

said smiling. 'Goodness, those are very pale children! Where did you find them? On the moon?' She laughed at them, loud happy laughter, as she got to her feet and began to lead the way to a little hut made of palm-leaves. 'Come in, come in and share our dinner. You're all as welcome as sunlight.'

Jane and Michael were about to follow, but Mary Poppins held them back.

'We've no time to stay, unfortunately. Just dropped in as we were passing, you know. We've got to get round the world,' she explained. And the black people flung up their hands in surprise.

'That's some distance, Mary Poppins,' said the man, his dark eyes looking doubtful as he rubbed his cheek with the end of the big club he was carrying.

'Round the *world*! That's all the way from here to there! You'll wear out your shoes,' his wife cried. She laughed again as if this, and everything else in the world were one huge happy joke. And while she was laughing Mary Poppins moved the compass and cried in a loud, firm voice, 'East!'

The world went spinning again and presently – it seemed to the astonished children only a few seconds – the palm-trees were no longer there, and when the spinning movement ceased they found themselves in a street lined with curiously shaped and very small houses. These appeared to be made of paper and the curved roofs were hung with little bells that rang gently in the breeze. Over the houses almond and plum trees spread branches weighted down with bright blossom, and along the little street people in strange flowery garments were quietly walking. It was a most pleasant and peaceful scene.

'I believe we're in China,' whispered Jane to Michael. 'Yes, I'm *sure* we are!' she went on, as they watched the door of one of the little paper houses opening and an old man stepping through it. He was curiously dressed, in a stiff brocade kimono of gold, and silken trousers gathered in with a golden ring at the ankles. His shoes turned up at the toes, very stylishly; from his head there hung a long grey pigtail that reached nearly to his knees, and from his lips drooped as far as his waist a very long moustache.

The old gentleman, seeing the little group formed by Mary Poppins and the children, bowed so low that his head touched the ground. Jane and Michael were surprised to see Mary Poppins bowing in the same way, till the daisies in her hat were brushing the earth.

'Where are your manners?' hissed Mary Poppins, looking up at them from that unusual position. And she said it so fiercely that they thought they had better bow, too, and the Twins bent their foreheads against the edge of their perambulator.

The old man, rising ceremoniously, began to speak.

'Honourable Mary of the House of Poppins,' he said. 'Deign to shed upon my unworthy abode the light of your virtuous countenance. And, I beseech you, lead thither to its graceless hearth these other honourable travellers.' He made another bow and waved his hand towards his house.

Jane and Michael had never heard such strange and beautiful language and were very astonished. But much more so when Mary Poppins herself answered the invitation with equal ceremony.

'Gracious Sir,' she began, 'it is with deep regret that we, the humblest of your acquaintance, must refuse your expansive and more-than-royal invitation. The lamb does not leave the ewe, nor the young bird its nest, more unwillingly than we depart from your shining presence. But, noble and ten-times-splendid Sir, we are in the act of encompassing the world and our visit to your honourable city can, alas, be but momentary. Permit us, therefore, to remove our unworthy persons from you without further ceremony.'

The Mandarin, for such indeed he was, bent his head and was preparing another elaborate bow, when Mary Poppins very quickly moved the compass again.

'West!' she said firmly.

Round went the world till Jane and Michael were quite dizzy. And when it grew still again they found themselves hurrying with Mary Poppins through great pine woods towards a clearing where several tents were pitched round a huge fire. In and out of the firelight flickered dark figures crowned with feathers and wearing loose tunics and trousers of fringed doe-skin. One of the largest of these figures broke away from the rest and came hurrying towards Mary Poppins and the children.

'Morning-Star-Mary,' he said. 'Greeting!' And he bent over her and touched his forehead with hers. Then he turned to the four children and did the same to them.

'My wigwam awaits you,' he said in a grave, friendly voice. 'We are just frying a reindeer for supper.'

'Chief Sun-at-Noonday,' said Mary Poppins, 'we have only dropped in – indeed, we have come, as it were, to say good-bye. We have been round the world and this is our last port of call.'

'Ha? Is that so?' said the Chief, looking very interested. 'I have often thought of doing that myself. But surely you can spend a little time with us, if only so long as to let this young person' (he nodded at Michael) 'try his strength against my great-great-great-grandson, Fleet-as-the-Wind!' The Chief clapped his hands.

'Hi – ho – hee!' he called loudly, and from the tents a little Indian boy ran towards them. He came swiftly up to Michael and when he reached him he flicked him lightly on the shoulder.

'Touched you last!' he said and ran like a hare.

That was too much for Michael. With a bound he was after him, with Jane on the heels of both. The three of them went dodging among the trees, circling one huge pine again and again as Fleet-as-the-Wind led them on, always laughing and always out of reach. Jane dropped behind, beaten, but Michael was angry now and set his teeth and fled screaming after Fleet-as-the-Wind, determined not to be outrun by an Indian boy.

'I'll get you!' he cried, straining to run still faster.

'What *are* you doing?' inquired Mary Poppins, snappily.

Michael looked back at her and stopped suddenly in his tracks. Then he turned again to the chase, but to his surprise there was no sign of Fleet-as-the-Wind. Nor of the Chief, nor the tents, nor the fire. There was not even a pine tree to be seen. Nothing but a garden seat, and Jane and the Twins and Mary Poppins standing in the middle of the Park.

'Running round and round that garden seat as if you'd gone mad! One'd think you'd been naughty *enough* for *one* day. Come along!' said Mary Poppins.

Michael pushed out his mouth sulkily.

'All round the world and back again in a minute – what a wonderful box!' Jane was saying happily.

'Give me my compass!' demanded Michael rudely.

'*My* compass, thank you,' said Mary Poppins, and she put it away in her pocket.

Michael looked at her as if he would like to kill her, and, indeed, what he felt was very like what he looked. But he just shrugged his shoulders and stalked off in front of them all and would not say a word to anybody.

'I could beat that boy any day,' he assured himself as he went through the gate of Number Seventeen and up the stairs . . .

The burning weight still hung heavily within him. After the adventure with the compass it seemed to grow worse, and towards the evening he grew naughtier and naughtier. He pinched the Twins when Mary Poppins was not looking, and when they cried he said in a falsely kind voice:

'Why, darlings, what *is* the matter?'

But Mary Poppins was not deceived by it.

'You've got something coming to you!' she said significantly. But the burning thing inside him would not let him care. He just shrugged his shoulders and pulled

Jane's hair. And after that he went to the supper table and upset his bread-and-milk.

'And that,' said Mary Poppins, 'is the end. Such deliberate naughtiness I never saw. In all my born days I never did, and that's a fact. Off you go! Straight into bed with you and not another word!' He had never seen her look so terrible.

But still he didn't care.

He went into the Night-nursery and undressed. No, he didn't care. He was bad, and if they didn't look out he'd be worse. He *didn't* care. He hated everybody. If they weren't careful he would run away and join a circus. There! Off went a button. Good – there would be fewer to do up in the morning. And another! All the better. Nothing in all the world could ever make him feel sorry. He would get into bed without brushing his hair or his teeth – certainly without saying his prayers.

He was just about to get into bed and, indeed, had one foot already in it, when he noticed the compass lying on the top of the chest of drawers.

Very slowly he withdrew his foot and tiptoed across the room. He knew now what he would do. He would take the compass and spin it and go round the world. And they'd never find him again. And it would serve them right. Without making a sound he lifted the chair and put it against the chest of drawers. Then he climbed up on it and took the compass in his hand.

He moved it.

'North, South, East, West!' he said very quickly, in case anybody should come in before he got well away.

A noise behind the chair startled him and he turned round guiltily, expecting to see Mary Poppins. But instead, there were four gigantic figures bearing down towards him – the Eskimo with a spear, the Negro Lady with her husband's huge club, the Mandarin with a great curved sword, and the Red Indian with a tomahawk. They were rushing upon him from all four quarters of the room with their weapons raised above their heads, and, instead of looking kind and friendly as they had done that afternoon, they now seemed threatening and full of revenge. They were almost on top of him, their huge, terrible, angry faces looming nearer and nearer. He felt their hot breath on his face and saw their weapons tremble in their hands.

With a cry Michael dropped the compass.

'Mary Poppins, Mary Poppins – help me, help me!' he screamed, and shut his eyes tight.

He felt something envelop him, something soft and warm. Oh, what was it? The fur coat of the Eskimo, the Mandarin's cloak, the Red Indian's doe-skin tunic, the black lady's feathers? Which of them had caught him? Oh, if only he had been good – if only!

'Mary Poppins!' he wailed, as he felt himself carried through the air and set down in something still softer.

'Oh, *dear* Mary Poppins!'

'All right, all right. I'm not deaf, I'm thankful to say – no need to shout,' he heard her saying calmly.

He opened one eye. He could see no sign of the four gigantic figures of the compass. He opened the other eye to make sure. No – not a glint of any of them. He sat up. He looked round the room. There was nothing there.

Then he discovered that the soft thing that was round him was his own blanket, and the soft thing he was lying on was his own bed. And oh, the heavy burning thing that had been inside him all day had melted and disappeared. He felt peaceful and happy, and as if he would like to give everybody he knew a birthday present.

'What – what happened?' he said rather anxiously to Mary Poppins.

'I told you that was my compass, didn't I? Be kind enough not to touch my things, *if* you please,' was all she said as she stooped and picked up the compass and put it in her pocket. Then she began to fold the clothes that he had thrown down on the floor.

'Shall I do it?' he said.

'No, thank you.'

He watched her go into the next room, and presently she returned and put something warm into his hands. It was a cup of milk.

Michael sipped it, tasting every drop several times with his tongue, making it last as long as possible so that Mary Poppins should stay beside him.

She stood there without saying a word, watching the milk slowly disappear. He could smell her crackling white apron and the faint flavour of toast that always hung about her so deliciously. But try as he would, he could not make the milk last for ever, and presently, with a sigh of regret, he handed her the empty cup and slipped down into the bed. He had never known it be so comfortable, he thought.

And he thought, too, how warm he was and how happy he felt and how lucky he was to be alive.

'Isn't it a funny thing, Mary Poppins,' he said drowsily, 'I've been so very naughty and I feel so very good.'

'Humph!' said Mary Poppins as she tucked him in and went away to wash up the supper things . . .

CHAPTER 7

The Bird Woman

'Perhaps she won't be there,' said Michael.

'Yes, she will,' said Jane. 'She's always there for ever and ever.'

They were walking up Ludgate Hill on the way to pay a visit to Mr Banks in the City. For he had said that morning to Mrs Banks:

'My dear, if it doesn't rain I think Jane and Michael might call for me at the Office to-day – that is, if you are agreeable. I have a feeling I should like to be taken to Tea and Shortbread Fingers and it's not often I have a Treat.'

And Mrs Banks had said she would think about it.

But all day long, though Jane and Michael had watched her anxiously, she had not seemed to be thinking about it at all. From the things she said, she was thinking about the Laundry Bill and Michael's new overcoat and where was Aunt Flossie's address, and why did that wretched Mrs Jackson ask her to tea on the second Thursday of the month when she knew that was the very day Mrs Banks had to go to the Dentist's?

Suddenly, when they felt quite sure she would never think about Mr Banks' treat, she said:

'Now, children, don't stand staring at me like that. Get your things on. You are going to the City to have tea with your Father. Had you forgotten?'

As if they could have forgotten! For it was not as though it were only the Tea that mattered. There was also the Bird Woman, and she herself was the best of all Treats.

That is why they were walking up Ludgate Hill and feeling very excited.

Mary Poppins walked between them, wearing her new hat and looking very distinguished. Every now and then she would look into the shop window just to make sure the hat was still there and that the pink roses on it had not turned into common flowers like marigolds.

Every time she stopped to make sure, Jane and Michael would sigh, but they did not dare say anything for fear she would spend even longer looking at herself in the windows, and turning this way and that to see which attitude was the most becoming.

But at last they came to St Paul's Cathedral, which was built a long time ago by a man with a bird's name. Wren it was, but he was no relation to Jenny. That is why so many birds live near Sir Christopher Wren's Cathedral, which also belongs to St Paul, and that is why the Bird Woman lives there, too.

'There she is!' cried Michael suddenly, and he danced on his toes with excitement.

'Don't point,' said Mary Poppins, giving a last glance at the pink roses in the window of a carpet-shop.

'She's saying it! She's saying it!' cried Jane, holding tight to herself for fear she would break in two with delight.

And she *was* saying it. The Bird Woman was there and she was saying it.

'Feed the Birds, Tuppence a Bag! Feed the Birds, Tup-

pence a Bag! Feed the Birds, Feed the Birds, Tuppence a
Bag, Tuppence a Bag!' Over and over again, the same
thing, in a high chanting voice that made the words seem
like a song.

And as she said it she held out little bags of bread-
crumbs to the passers-by.

All round her flew the birds, circling and leaping and
swooping and rising. Mary Poppins always called them
'sparrers' because, she said conceitedly, all birds were alike
to her. But Jane and Michael knew that they were not
sparrows, but doves and pigeons. There were fussy and
chatty grey doves like Grandmothers; and brown, rough-
voiced pigeons like Uncles; and greeny, cackling, no-I've-
no-money-to-day pigeons like Fathers. And the silly,
anxious, soft blue doves were like Mothers. That's what
Jane and Michael thought, anyway.

They flew round and round the head of the Bird
Woman as the children approached, and then, as though
to tease her, they suddenly rushed away through the air
and sat on the top of St Paul's, laughing and turning their
heads away and pretending they didn't know her.

It was Michael's turn to buy a bag. Jane had bought one
last time. He walked up to the Bird Woman and held out
four halfpennies.

'*Feed* the Birds, Tuppence a Bag!' said the Bird Woman,
as she put a bag of crumbs into his hand and tucked the
money away into the folds of her huge black skirt.

'Why don't you have penny bags?' said Michael. 'Then
I could buy two.'

'Feed the Birds, *Tuppence* a Bag!' said the Bird Woman,

and Michael knew it was no good asking her any more questions. He and Jane had often tried, but all she could say, and all she had ever been able to say, was, 'Feed the Birds, Tuppence a Bag!' Just as a cuckoo can only say 'Cuckoo,' no matter what questions you ask him.

Jane and Michael and Mary Poppins spread the crumbs in a circle on the ground, and presently, one by one at first, and then in twos and threes, the birds came down from St Paul's.

'Dainty David,' said Mary Poppins with a sniff, as one bird picked up a crumb and dropped it again from its beak.

But the other birds swarmed upon the food, pushing and scrambling and shouting. At last there wasn't a crumb left, for it is not really polite for a pigeon or a dove to leave anything on the plate. When they were quite certain that the meal was finished the birds rose with one grand, fluttering movement and flew round the Bird Woman's head, copying in their own language the words she said. One of them sat on her hat and pretended he was a decoration for the crown. And another of them mistook Mary Poppins' new hat for a rose-garden and pecked off a flower.

'You sparrer!' cried Mary Poppins, and shook her umbrella at him. The pigeon, very offended, flew back to the Bird Woman, and to pay out Mary Poppins, stuck the rose in the ribbon of the Bird Woman's hat.

'You ought to be in a pie – that's where *you* ought to be,' said Mary Poppins to him very angrily. Then she called to Jane and Michael.

'Time to go,' she said, and flung a parting glance of fury at the pigeon. But he only laughed and flicked his tail and turned his back on her.

'Good-bye,' said Michael to the Bird Woman.

'Feed the Birds,' she replied, smiling.

'Good-bye,' said Jane.

'Tuppence a Bag!' said the Bird Woman and waved her hand.

They left her then, walking one on either side of Mary Poppins.

'What happens when *everybody* goes away – like us?' said Michael to Jane.

He knew quite well what happened, but it was the proper thing to ask Jane because the story was really hers.

So Jane told him and he added the bits she had forgotten.

'At night when everybody goes to bed –' began Jane.

'And the stars come out,' added Michael.

'Yes, and even if they don't – all the birds come down from the top of St Paul's and run very carefully all over the ground just to see there are no crumbs left, and to tidy it up for the morning. And when they have done that –'

'You've forgotten the baths.'

'Oh, yes – they bath themselves and comb their wings with their claws. And when they have done that they fly three times round the head of the Bird Woman and then they settle.'

'Do they sit on her shoulders?'

'Yes, and on her hat.'

'And on her basket with the bags in it?'

'Yes, and some on her knee. Then she smooths down the head-feathers of each one in turn and tells it to be a good bird –'

'In the bird language?'

'Yes. And when they are all sleepy and don't want to stay awake any longer, she spreads out her skirts, as a mother hen spreads out her wings and the birds go creep, creep, creeping underneath. And as soon as the last one is under she settles down over them, making little brooding, nesting noises and they sleep there till morning.'

Michael sighed happily. He loved the story and was never tired of hearing it.

'And it's all quite true, isn't it?' he said, just as he always did.

'No,' said Mary Poppins, who always said 'No.'

'Yes,' said Jane, who always knew everything . . .

CHAPTER 8

Mrs Corry

'Two pounds of sausages – Best Pork,' said Mary Poppins. 'And at once, please. We're in a hurry.'

The Butcher, who wore a large blue-and-white striped apron, was a fat and friendly man. He was also large and red and rather like one of his own sausages. He leant upon his chopping-block and gazed admiringly at Mary Poppins. Then he winked pleasantly at Jane and Michael.

'In a Nurry?' he said to Mary Poppins. 'Well, that's a pity. I'd hoped you'd dropped in for a bit of a chat. We Butchers, you know, like a bit of company. And we don't often get the chance of talking to a nice, handsome young lady like you – ' He broke off suddenly, for he had caught sight of Mary Poppins' face. The expression on it was awful. And the Butcher found himself wishing there was a trap-door in the floor of his shop that would open and swallow him up.

'Oh, well – ' he said, blushing even redder than usual. 'If you're in a Nurry, of course. Two pounds, did you say? Best Pork? Right you are!'

And he hurriedly hooked down a long strip of the sausages that were festooned across the shop. He cut off a length – about three-quarters of a yard – wound it into a sort of garland, and wrapped it up first in white and then in brown paper. He pushed the parcel across the chopping-block.

'*AND* the next?' he said hopefully, still blushing.

'There will be *no* next,' said Mary Poppins, with a haughty sniff. And she took the sausages and turned the perambulator round very quickly, and wheeled it out of the shop in such a way that the Butcher knew he had mortally offended her. But she glanced at the window as she went so that she could see how her new shoes looked reflected in it. They were bright brown kid with two buttons, very smart.

Jane and Michael trailed after her, wondering when she would have come to the end of her shopping-list but, because of the look on her face, not daring to ask her.

Mary Poppins gazed up and down the street as if deep in thought, and then, suddenly making up her mind, she snapped:

'Fishmonger!' and turned the perambulator in at the shop next to the Butcher's.

'One Dover Sole, pound and a half of Halibut, pint of Prawns and a Lobster,' said Mary Poppins, talking so quickly that only somebody used to taking such orders could possibly have understood her.

The Fishmonger, unlike the Butcher, was a long thin man, so thin that he seemed to have no front to him but only two sides. And he looked so sad that you felt he had either just been weeping or was just going to. Jane said that this was due to some secret sorrow that had haunted him since his youth, and Michael thought that the Fishmonger's Mother must have fed him entirely on bread

and water when he was a baby, and that he had never forgotten it.

'Anything else?' said the Fishmonger hopelessly, in a
voice that suggested he was quite sure there wouldn't be.

'Not to-day,' said Mary Poppins.

The Fishmonger shook his head sadly and did not look
at all surprised. He had known all along there would be
nothing else.

Sniffing gently, he tied up the parcel and dropped it into
the perambulator.

'Bad weather,' he observed, wiping his eye with his hand.
'Don't believe we're going to get any summer at all – not
that we ever did, of course. *You* don't look too blooming,'
he said to Mary Poppins. 'But then, nobody does –'

Mary Poppins tossed her head.

'Speak for yourself,' she said crossly, and flounced to
the door, pushing the perambulator so fiercely that it
bumped into a bag of oysters.

'The idea!' Jane and Michael heard her say as she glanced
down at her shoes. Not looking too blooming in her new
brown kid shoes with two buttons – the idea! That was
what they heard her thinking.

Outside on the pavement she paused, looking at her list
and ticking off what she had bought. Michael stood first
on one leg and then on the other.

'Mary Poppins, are we *never* going home?' he said crossly.

Mary Poppins turned and regarded him with something like disgust.

'That,' she said briefly, 'is as it may be.' And Michael,
watching her fold up her list, wished he had not spoken.

'*You* can go home, if you like,' she said haughtily. '*We* are going to buy the gingerbread.'

Michael's face fell. If only he had managed to say nothing! He hadn't known that Gingerbread was at the end of the list.

'That's your way,' said Mary Poppins shortly, pointing in the direction of Cherry Tree Lane. 'If you don't get lost,' she added as an afterthought.

'Oh no, Mary Poppins, *please*, no! I didn't mean it, really. I – oh – Mary Poppins, please – ' cried Michael.

'Do let him come, Mary Poppins!' said Jane. 'I'll push the perambulator if only you'll let him come.'

Mary Poppins sniffed. 'If it wasn't Friday,' she said darkly to Michael, 'you'd go home in a twink – in an absolute Twink!'

She moved onwards, pushing John and Barbara. Jane and Michael knew that she had relented, and followed wondering what a Twink was. Suddenly Jane noticed that they were going in the wrong direction.

'But, Mary Poppins, I thought you said gingerbread – this isn't the way to Green, Brown and Johnson's, where we always get it – ' she began, and stopped because of Mary Poppins' face.

'Am I doing the shopping or are you?' Mary Poppins inquired.

'You,' said Jane, in a very small voice.

'Oh, really? I thought it was the other way round,' said Mary Poppins with a scornful laugh.

She gave the perambulator a little twist with her hand and it turned a corner and drew up suddenly. Jane and

Michael, stopping abruptly behind it, found themselves outside the most curious shop they had ever seen. It was very small and very dingy. Faded loops of coloured paper hung in the windows, and on the shelves were shabby little boxes of Sherbet, old Liquorice Sticks, and very withered, very hard Apples-on-a-stick. There was a small dark doorway between the windows, and through this Mary Poppins propelled the perambulator while Jane and Michael followed at her heels.

Inside the shop they could dimly see the glass-topped counter that ran round three sides of it. And in a case under the glass were rows and rows of dark, dry gingerbread, each slab so studded with gilt stars that the shop itself seemed to be faintly lit by them. Jane and Michael glanced round to find out what kind of a person was to serve them, and were very surprised when Mary Poppins called out:

'Fannie! Annie! Where are you?' Her voice seemed to echo back to them from each dark wall of the shop.

And as she called, two of the largest people the children had ever seen rose from behind the counter and shook hands with Mary Poppins. The huge women then leant down over the counter and said, 'How de do?' in voices as large as themselves, and shook hands with Jane and Michael.

'How do you do, Miss – ?' Michael paused, wondering which of the large ladies was which.

'Fannie's my name,' said one of them. 'My rheumatism is about the same; thank you for asking.' She spoke very

mournfully, as though she were unused to such a court-
eous greeting.

'It's a lovely day – 'began Jane politely to the other sister,
who kept Jane's hand imprisoned for almost a minute in
her huge clasp.

'I'm Annie,' she informed them miserably. 'And handsome is as handsome does.'

Jane and Michael thought that both the sisters had a
very odd way of expressing themselves, but they had not
time to be surprised for long, for Miss Fannie and Miss
Annie were reaching out their long arms to the perambulator. Each shook hands solemnly with one of theTwins,
who were so astonished that they began to cry.

'Now, now, now, now! What's this, what's this?' A high,
thin, crackly little voice came from the back of the shop.
At the sound of it the expression on the faces of Miss
Fannie and Miss Annie, sad before, became even sadder.
They seemed frightened and ill at ease, and somehow Jane
and Michael realised that the two huge sisters were wishing that they were much smaller and less conspicuous.

'What's all this I hear?' cried the curious high little
voice, coming nearer. And presently, round the corner
of the glass case the owner of it appeared. She was as
small as her voice and as crackly, and to the children she
seemed to be older than anything in the world, with her
wispy hair and her stick-like legs and her wizened,
wrinkled little face. But in spite of this she ran towards
them as lightly and as gaily as though she were still a
young girl.

'Now, now, now – well, I do declare! Bless me if it isn't

Mary Poppins, with John and Barbara Banks. What – Jane and Michael, too? Well, isn't this a nice surprise for me? I assure you I haven't been so surprised since Christopher Columbus discovered America – truly I haven't!'

She smiled delightedly as she came to greet them, and her feet made little dancing movements inside the tiny elastic-sided boots. She ran to the perambulator and rocked it gently, crooking her thin, twisted, old fingers at John and Barbara until they stopped crying and began to laugh.

'That's better!' she said, cackling gaily. Then she did a very odd thing. She broke off two of her fingers and gave one each to John and Barbara. And the oddest part of it was that in the space left by the broken-off fingers two new ones grew at once. Jane and Michael clearly saw it happen.

'Only Barley-Sugar – can't possibly hurt 'em,' the old lady said to Mary Poppins.

'Anything *you* give them, Mrs Corry, could only do them good,' said Mary Poppins with most surprising courtesy.

'What a pity,' Michael couldn't help saying, 'they weren't Peppermint Bars.'

'Well, they are, sometimes,' said Mrs Corry gleefully, 'and very good they taste, too. I often nibble 'em myself, if I can't sleep at night. Splendid for the digestion.'

'What will they be next time?' asked Jane, looking at Mrs Corry's fingers with interest.

'Aha!' said Mrs Corry. 'That's just the question. I never know from day to day what they will be. I take the chance, my dear, as I heard William the Conqueror say to his Mother when she advised him not to go conquering England.'

'You must be *very* old!' said Jane, sighing enviously, and wondering if she would ever be able to remember what Mrs Corry remembered.

Mrs Corry flung back her wispy little head and shrieked with laughter.

'Old!' she said. 'Why, I'm quite a chicken compared to my Grandmother. Now, there's an old woman *if* you like. Still, I go back a good way. I remember the time when they were making this world, anyway, and I was well out of my teens then. My goodness, that *was* a to-do, I can tell you!'

She broke off suddenly, screwing up her little eyes at the children.

'But, deary me – here am I running on and on and you not being served! I suppose, my dear' – she turned to Mary Poppins, whom she appeared to know very well – 'I suppose you've all come for some Gingerbread?'

'That's right, Mrs Corry,' said Mary Poppins politely.

'Good. Have Fannie and Annie given you any?' She looked at Jane and Michael as she said this.

Jane shook her head. Two hushed voices came from behind the counter.

'No, Mother,' said Miss Fannie meekly.

'We were just going to, Mother – ' began Miss Annie in a frightened whisper.

At that Mrs Corry drew herself up to her full height and regarded her gigantic daughters furiously. Then she said in a soft, fierce, terrifying voice:

'Just going to? Oh, *indeed*! That is *very* interesting. And who, may I ask, Annie, gave you permission to give away *my* gingerbread – ?'

'Nobody, Mother. And I didn't give it away. I only thought – '

'You only thought! That is *very* kind of you. But I will thank you not to think. *I* can do all the thinking that is necessary here!' said Mrs Corry in her soft, terrible voice. Then she burst into a harsh cackle of laughter.

'Look at her! Just look at her! Cowardy-custard! Cry-baby!' she shrieked, pointing her knotty finger at her daughter.

Jane and Michael turned and saw a large tear coursing

down Miss Annie's huge, sad face, but they did not like to say anything, for, in spite of her tininess, Mrs Corry made them feel rather small and frightened. But as soon as Mrs Corry looked the other way Jane seized the opportunity to offer Miss Annie her handkerchief. The huge tear completely drenched it, and Miss Annie, with a grateful look, wrung it out before she returned it to Jane.

'And you, Fannie – did *you* think, too, I wonder?' The high little voice was now directed at the other daughter.

'No, Mother,' said Miss Fannie trembling.

'Humph! Just as well for you! Open that case!'

With frightened, fumbling fingers, Miss Fannie opened the glass case.

'Now, my darlings,' said Mrs Corry in quite a different voice. She smiled and beckoned so sweetly to Jane and Michael that they were ashamed of having been frightened of her, and felt that she must be very nice after all. 'Won't you come and take your pick, my lambs? It's a special recipe to-day – one I got from Alfred the Great. He was a very good cook, I remember, though he did once burn the cakes. How many?'

Jane and Michael looked at Mary Poppins.

'Four each,' she said. 'That's twelve. One dozen.'

'I'll make it a Baker's Dozen – take thirteen,' said Mrs Corry cheerfully.

So Jane and Michael chose thirteen slabs of ginger-bread, each with its gilt paper star. Their arms were piled up with the delicious dark cakes. Michael could not resist nibbling a corner of one of them.

'Good?' squeaked Mrs Corry, and when he nodded she

picked up her skirts and did a few steps of the Highland Fling for pure pleasure.

'Hooray, hooray, splendid, hooray!' she cried in her shrill little voice. Then she came to a standstill and her face grew serious.

'But remember – I'm not *giving* them away. I must be paid. The price is threepence for each of you.'

Mary Poppins opened her purse and took out three threepenny-bits. She gave one each to Jane and Michael.

'Now,' said Mrs Corry. 'Stick 'em on my coat! That's where they all go.'

They looked closely at her long black coat. And sure enough they found it was studded with threepenny-bits as a Coster's coat is with pearl buttons.

'Come along. Stick 'em on!' repeated Mrs Corry, rubbing her hands with pleasant expectation. 'You'll find they won't drop off.'

Mary Poppins stepped forward and pressed her three-penny-bit against the collar of Mrs Corry's coat.

To the surprise of Jane and Michael, it stuck.

Then they put theirs on – Jane's on the right shoulder and Michael's on the front hem. Theirs stuck, too.

'How very extraordinary,' said Jane.

'Not at all, my dear,' said Mrs Corry chuckling. 'Or rather, not so extraordinary as other things I could mention.' And she winked largely at Mary Poppins.

'I'm afraid we must be off now, Mrs Corry,' said Mary Poppins. 'There is Baked Custard for lunch, and I must be home in time to make it. That Mrs Brill – '

'A poor cook?' inquired Mrs Corry interrupting.

'Poor!' said Mary Poppins contemptuously. '*That's* not the word.'

'Ah!' Mrs Corry put her finger alongside her nose and looked very wise. Then she said:

'Well, my dear Miss Poppins, it has been a very pleasant visit and I am sure my girls have enjoyed it as much as I have.' She nodded in the direction of her two large mournful daughters. 'And you'll come again soon, won't you, with Jane and Michael and the Babies? Now, are you sure you can carry the Gingerbread?' she continued, turning to Michael and Jane.

They nodded. Mrs Corry drew closer to them, with a curious, important, inquisitive look on her face.

'I wonder,' she said dreamily, 'what you will do with the paper stars?'

'Oh, we'll keep them,' said Jane. 'We always do.'

'Ah – you keep them! And I wonder *where* you keep them?' Mrs Corry's eyes were half closed and she looked more inquisitive than ever.

'Well,' Jane began. 'Mine are all under my handkerchiefs in the top left-hand drawer and –'

'Mine are in a shoe-box on the bottom shelf of the wardrobe,' said Michael.

'Top left-hand drawer and shoe-box in the wardrobe,' said Mrs Corry thoughtfully, as though she were committing the words to memory. Then she gave Mary Poppins a long look and nodded her head slightly. Mary Poppins nodded slightly in return. It seemed as if some secret had passed between them.

'Well,' said Mrs Corry brightly, 'that is very interesting.

You don't know how glad I am to know you keep your stars. I shall remember that. You see, I remember every-thing – even what Guy Fawkes had for dinner every second Sunday. And now, good-bye. Come again soon. Come again so-o-o-o-o-n!'

Mrs Corry's voice seemed to be growing fainter and fading away, and presently, without being quite aware of what happened, Jane and Michael found themselves on the pavement, walking behind Mary Poppins who was again examining her list.

They turned and looked behind them.

'Why, Jane,' said Michael with surprise, 'it's not there!'

'So I see,' said Jane, staring and staring.

And they were right. The shop was *not* there. It had en-tirely disappeared.

'How odd!' said Jane.

'Isn't it?' said Michael. 'But the Gingerbread is very good.'

And they were so busy biting their Gingerbread into different shapes – a man, a flower, a teapot – that they quite forgot how *very* odd it was.

They remembered it again that night, however, when the lights were out and they were both supposed to be sound asleep.

'Jane, Jane!' whispered Michael. 'I hear someone tip-toeing on the stairs – listen!'

'Sssh!' hissed Jane from her bed, for she, too, had heard the footsteps.

Presently the door opened with a little click and some-body came into the room. It was Mary Poppins, dressed in hat and coat all ready to go out.

She moved about the room softly with quick secret movements. Jane and Michael watched her through half-closed eyes without stirring.

First she went to the chest-of-drawers, opened a drawer and shut it again after a moment. Then, on tip-toe, she went to the wardrobe, opened it, bent down and put something in or took something out (they couldn't tell which). Snap! The wardrobe door shut quickly and Mary Poppins hurried from the room.

Michael sat up in bed.

'What was she doing?' he said to Jane in a loud whisper.

'I don't know. Perhaps she's forgotten her gloves or her shoes or – ' Jane broke off suddenly. 'Michael, listen!'

He listened. From down below – in the garden, it seemed – they could hear several voices whispering together, very earnestly and excitedly.

With a quick movement Jane got out of bed and beck-oned Michael. They crept on bare feet to the window and looked down.

There, outside in the Lane, stood a tiny form and two gigantic figures.

'Mrs Corry and Miss Fannie and Miss Annie,' said Jane in a whisper.

And so indeed it was. It was a curious group. Mrs Corry was looking through the bars of the gate of Number Seventeen. Miss Fannie had two long ladders balanced on one huge shoulder, while Miss Annie appeared to be carrying in one hand a large pail of something that looked like glue and in the other an enormous paint-brush.

From where they stood, hidden by the curtain, Jane and Michael could distinctly hear their voices.

'She's late!' Mrs Corry was saying crossly and anxiously.

'Perhaps,' Miss Fannie began timidly, settling the ladders more firmly on her shoulder, 'one of the children is ill and she couldn't – '

'Get away in time,' said Miss Annie, nervously completing her sister's sentence.

'Silence!' said Mrs Corry fiercely, and Jane and Michael distinctly heard her whisper something about 'great galumphing giraffes,' and they knew she was referring to her unfortunate daughters.

'Hist!' said Mrs Corry suddenly, listening with her head on one side, like a small bird.

There was the sound of the front door being quietly opened and shut again, and the creak of footsteps on the path. Mrs Corry smiled and waved her hand as Mary Poppins came to meet them, carrying a market basket on her arm, and in the basket was something that seemed to give out a faint, mysterious light.

'Come along, come along, we must hurry! We haven't much time,' said Mrs Corry, taking Mary Poppins by the arm. 'Look lively, you two!' And she moved off, followed by Miss Fannie and Miss Annie, who were obviously trying to look as lively as possible but not succeeding very well. They tramped heavily after their Mother and Mary Poppins, bending under their loads.

Jane and Michael saw all four of them go down Cherry

Tree Lane, and then they turned a little to the left and went up the hill. When they got to the top of the hill, where there were no houses but only grass and clover, they stopped.

Miss Annie put down her pail of glue, and Miss Fannie swung the ladders from her shoulder and steadied them until both stood in an upright position. Then she held one and Miss Annie the other.

'What on earth are they going to do?' said Michael, gaping. But there was no need for Jane to reply, for he could see for himself what was happening.

As soon as Miss Fannie and Miss Annie had so fixed the ladders that they seemed to be standing with one end on the earth and the other leaning on the sky, Mrs Corry picked up her skirts and the paint-brush in one hand and the pail of glue in the other. Then she set her foot on the lowest rung of one of the ladders and began to climb it. Mary Poppins, carrying her basket, climbed the other.

Then Jane and Michael saw a most amazing sight. As soon as she arrived at the top of her ladder, Mrs Corry dipped her brush into the glue and began slapping the sticky substance against the sky. And Mary Poppins, when this had been done, took something shiny from her basket and fixed it to the glue. When she took her hand away they saw that she was sticking the Gingerbread Stars to the sky. As each one was placed in position it began to twinkle furiously, sending out rays of sparkling golden light.

'They're ours!' said Michael breathlessly. 'They're our

stars. She thought we were asleep and came in and took them!'

But Jane was silent. She was watching Mrs Corry splashing the glue on the sky and Mary Poppins sticking on the stars and Miss Fannie and Miss Annie moving the ladders to a new position as the spaces in the sky became filled up.

At last it was over. Mary Poppins shook out her basket and showed Mrs Corry that there was nothing left in it. Then they came down from the ladders and the procession started down the hill again, Miss Fannie shouldering the ladders, Miss Annie jangling her empty glue pail. At the corner they stood talking for a moment; then Mary Poppins shook hands with them all and hurried up the Lane again. Mrs Corry, dancing lightly in her elastic-sided boots and holding her skirts daintily with her hands, disappeared in the other direction with her huge daughters stumping noisily behind her.

The garden-gate clicked. Footsteps creaked on the path. The front door opened and shut with a soft clanging sound. Presently they heard Mary Poppins come quietly up the stairs, tip-toe past the nursery and go on into the room where she slept with John and Barbara.

As the sound of her footsteps died away, Jane and Michael looked at each other. Then without a word they went together to the top left-hand drawer and looked.

There was nothing there but a pile of Jane's handkerchiefs.

'I told you so,' said Michael.

One end on the earth and the other leaning on the sky

Next they went to the wardrobe and looked into the shoe-box. It was empty.

'But how? But why?' said Michael, sitting down on the edge of his bed and staring at Jane.

Jane said nothing. She just sat beside him with her arms round her knees and thought and thought and thought. At last she shook back her hair and stretched herself and stood up.

'What *I* want to know,' she said, 'is this: Are the stars gold paper or is the gold paper stars?'

There was no reply to her question and she did not expect one. She knew that only somebody very much wiser than Michael could give her the right answer . . .

CHAPTER 9

John and Barbara's Story

Jane and Michael had gone off to a party, wearing their best clothes and looking, as Ellen the housemaid said when she saw them, 'just like a shop window.'

All the afternoon the house was very quiet and still, as though it were thinking its own thoughts, or dreaming perhaps.

Down in the kitchen Mrs Brill was reading the paper with her spectacles perched on her nose. Robertson Ay was sitting in the garden busily doing nothing. Mrs Banks was on the drawing-room sofa with her feet up. And the house stood very quietly around them all, dreaming its own dreams, or thinking perhaps.

Upstairs in the nursery Mary Poppins was airing the clothes by the fire, and the sunlight poured in at the window, flickering on the white walls, dancing over the cots where the babies were lying.

'I say, move over! You're right in my eyes,' said John in a loud voice.

'Sorry!' said the sunlight. 'But I can't help it. I've got to get across this room somehow. Orders is orders. I must move from East to West in a day and my way lies through this Nursery. Sorry! Shut your eyes and you won't notice me.'

The gold shaft of sunlight lengthened across the room.

It was obviously moving as quickly as it could in order to oblige John.

'How soft, how sweet you are! I love you,' said Barbara holding out her hands to its shining warmth.

'Good girl,' said the sunlight approvingly, and moved up over her cheeks and into her hair with a light, caressing movement. 'Do you like the feel of me?' it said, as though it loved being praised.

'Dee-licious!' said Barbara, with a happy sigh.

'Chatter, chatter, chatter! I never heard such a place for chatter. There's always somebody talking in this room,' said a shrill voice at the window.

John and Barbara looked up.

It was the Starling who lived on the top of the chimney.

'I like that,' said Mary Poppins, turning round quickly.

'What about yourself? All day long – yes, and half the night, too, on the roofs and telegraph poles. Roaring and screaming and shouting – you'd talk the leg off a chair, you would. Worse than any sparrer, and that's the truth.'

The Starling cocked his head on one side and looked down at her from his perch on the window-frame.

'Well,' he said, 'I have my business to attend to. Consultations, discussions, arguments, bargaining. And that, of course, necessitates a certain amount of – er – quiet conversation – '

'Quiet!' exclaimed John, laughing heartily.

'And I wasn't talking to you, young man,' said the Starling, hopping down on to the window-sill. 'And *you* needn't talk – anyway. I heard you for several hours on end last Saturday week. Goodness, I thought you'd never stop – you kept me awake all night.'

'That wasn't talking,' said John. 'I was – ' He paused. 'I mean, I had a pain.'

'Humph!' said the Starling, and hopped on to the railing of Barbara's cot. He sidled along it until he came to the head of the cot. Then he said in a soft, wheedling voice:

'Well, Barbara B., anything for the old fellow to-day, eh?'

Barbara pulled herself into a sitting position by holding on to one of the bars of her cot.

'There's the other half of my arrowroot biscuit,' she said, and held it out in her round, fat fist.

The Starling swooped down, plucked it out of her hand and flew back to the window-sill. He began nibbling it greedily.

'Thank you!' said Mary Poppins, meaningly, but the Starling was too busy eating to notice the rebuke.

'I said "Thank you!"' said Mary Poppins a little louder. The Starling looked up.

'Eh – what? Oh, get along, girl, get along. I've no time for such frills and furbelows.' And he gobbled up the last of his biscuit.

The room was very quiet.

John, drowsing in the sunlight, put the toes of his right foot into his mouth and ran them along the place where his teeth were just beginning to come through.

'Why do you bother to do that?' said Barbara, in her soft, amused voice that seemed always to be full of laughter. 'There's nobody to see you.'

'I know,' said John, playing a tune on his toes. 'But I like to keep in practice. It *does* so amuse the Grown-ups. Did you notice that Aunt Flossie nearly went mad with delight when I did it yesterday? "The Darling, the Clever, the Marvel, the Creature!" – didn't you hear her saying all that?' And John threw his foot from him and roared with laughter as he thought of Aunt Flossie.

'She liked my trick, too,' said Barbara complacently. 'I took off both my socks and she said I was so sweet she would like to eat me. Isn't it funny – when *I* say I'd like to eat something I really mean it. Biscuits and Rusks and the knobs of beds and so on. But Grown-ups never mean what they say, it seems to me. She couldn't have *really* wanted to eat me, could she?'

'No. It's only the idiotic way they have of talking,' said John. 'I don't believe I'll ever understand Grown-ups. They all seem so stupid. And even Jane and Michael are stupid sometimes.'

'Um,' agreed Barbara, thoughtfully pulling off her socks and putting them on again.

'For instance,' John went on, 'they don't understand a single thing we say. But, worse than that, they don't understand what *other* things say. Why, only last Monday I heard Jane remark that she wished she knew what language the Wind spoke.'

'I know,' said Barbara. 'It's astonishing. And Michael always insists – haven't you heard him? – that the Starling says "Wee-Twe – ee – ee!" He seems not to know that the Starling says nothing of the kind, but speaks exactly the same language as we do. Of course, one doesn't expect Mother and Father to know about it – they don't know *anything*, though they *are* such darlings – but you'd think Jane and Michael would – '

'They did once,' said Mary Poppins, folding up one of Jane's nightgowns.

'What?' said John and Barbara together in very surprised voices. 'Really? You mean they understood the Starling and the Wind and – '

'And what the trees say and the language of the sunlight and the stars – of course they did! *Once*,' said Mary Poppins.

'But – how is it that they've forgotten it all?' said John, wrinkling up his forehead and trying to understand.

'Aha!' said the Starling knowingly, looking up from the remains of his biscuit. 'Wouldn't you like to know?'

'Because they've grown older,' explained Mary Poppins. 'Barbara, put on your socks at once, please.'

'That's a silly reason,' said John, looking sternly at her.

'It's the true one, then,' Mary Poppins said, tying Barbara's socks firmly round her ankles.

'Well, it's Jane and Michael who are silly,' John continued. 'I know *I* shan't forget when *I* get older.'

'Nor I,' said Barbara, contentedly sucking her finger.

'Yes, you will,' said Mary Poppins firmly.

The Twins sat up and looked at her.

'Huh!' said the Starling contemptuously. 'Look at 'em! They think they're the World's Wonders. Little miracles – I *don't* think! Of course you'll forget – same as Jane and Michael.'

'We *won't*,' said the Twins, looking at the Starling as if they would like to murder him.

The Starling jeered.

'I say you will,' he insisted. 'It isn't your fault, of course,' he added more kindly. 'You'll forget because you just can't help it. There never was a human being that remembered after the age of one – at the very latest – except, of course, Her.' And he jerked his head over his shoulder at Mary Poppins.

'But why can she remember and not us?' said John.

'A-a-a-h! She's different. She's the Great Exception. Can't go by *her*,' said the Starling, grinning at them both.

John and Barbara were silent.

The Starling went on explaining.

'She's something special, you see. Not in the matter of looks, of course. One of my own day-old chicks is handsomer than Mary P. ever was –'

'Here, you impertinence!' said Mary Poppins crossly, making a dart at him and flicking her apron in his direction. But the Starling leapt aside and flew up to the window-frame, whistling wickedly, well out of reach.

'Huh!' said the Starling. 'Look at 'em!'

'Thought you had me that time, didn't you?' he jeered
and shook his wing-feathers at her.

Mary Poppins snorted.

The sunlight moved on through the room, drawing its
long gold shaft after it. Outside a light wind had sprung
up and was whispering gently to the cherry trees in the
Lane.

'Listen, listen, the wind's talking,' said John, tilting his head on one side. 'Do you really mean we won't be able to hear *that* when we're older, Mary Poppins?'

'You'll hear all right,' said Mary Poppins, 'but you won't understand.' At that Barbara began to weep gently. There were tears in John's eyes, too. 'Well, it can't be helped. It's how things happen,' said Mary Poppins sensibly.

'Look at them, just look at them!' jeered the Starling. 'Crying fit to kill themselves! Why, a starling in the egg's got more sense. Look at them!'

For John and Barbara were now crying piteously in their cots – long-drawn sobs of deep unhappiness.

Suddenly the door opened and in came Mrs Banks.

'I thought I heard the babies,' she said. Then she ran to the Twins. 'What is it, my darlings? Oh, my Treasures, my Sweets, my Love-birds, what is it? Why are they crying so, Mary Poppins? They've been so quiet all the afternoon – not a sound out of them. What can be the matter?'

'Yes, ma'am. No, ma'am. I expect they're getting their teeth, ma'am,' said Mary Poppins, deliberately not looking in the direction of the Starling.

'Oh, of course – that must be it,' said Mrs Banks brightly.

'I don't want teeth if they make me forget all the things I like best,' wailed John, tossing about in his cot.

'Neither do I,' wept Barbara, burying her face in her pillow.

'My poor ones, my pets – it will be all right when the naughty old teeth come through,' said Mrs Banks soothingly, going from one cot to the other.

'You don't understand!' roared John furiously. 'I don't *want* teeth.'

'It won't be all right, it will be all *wrong*!' wailed Barbara to her pillow.

'Yes – yes. There – there. Mother knows – Mother understands. It will be all right when the teeth come through,' crooned Mrs Banks tenderly.

A faint noise came from the window. It was the Starling hurriedly swallowing a laugh. Mary Poppins gave him one look. That sobered him, and he continued to regard the scene without the hint of a smile.

Mrs Banks was patting her children gently, first one and then the other, and murmuring words that were meant to be reassuring. Suddenly John stopped crying. He had very good manners, and he was fond of his Mother and remembered what was due to her. It was not *her* fault, poor woman, that she always said the wrong thing. It was just, he reflected, that she did not understand. So, to show that he forgave her, he turned over on his back, and very dolefully, sniffing back his tears, he picked up his right foot in both hands and ran his toes along his open mouth.

'Clever One, oh, Clever One,' said his Mother admiringly. He did it again and she was very pleased.

Then Barbara, not to be outdone in courtesy, came out of her pillow and with her tears still wet on her iace, sat up and plucked off both her socks.

'Wonderful Girl,' said Mrs Banks proudly, and kissed her.

'There, you see, Mary Poppins! They're quite good again. I can always comfort them. Quite good, quite good,' said Mrs Banks, as though she were singing a lullaby. 'And the teeth will soon be through.'

'Yes, ma'am,' said Mary Poppins quietly; and smiling to the Twins, Mrs Banks went out and closed the door.

The moment she had disappeared the Starling burst into a peal of rude laughter.

'Excuse me smiling!' he cried. 'But really – I can't help it. What a scene! *What* a scene!'

John took no notice of him. He pushed his face through the bars of his cot and called softly and fiercely to Barbara:

'I *won't* be like the others. I tell you I won't. They,' he jerked his head towards the Starling and Mary Poppins, 'can say what they like. I'll never forget, *never*!'

Mary Poppins smiled, a secret, I-know-better-than-you sort of smile, all to herself.

'Nor I,' answered Barbara. 'Ever.'

'Bless my tail-feathers – listen to them!' shrieked the Starling, as he put his wings on his hips and roared with mirth. 'As if they could help forgetting! Why, in a month or two – three at the *most* – they won't even know what my name is – silly cuckoos! Silly, half-grown, featherless cuckoos! Ha! Ha! Ha!' And with another loud peal of laughter he spread his speckled wings and flew out of the window . . .

It was not very long afterwards that the teeth, after much trouble, came through as all teeth must, and the Twins had their first birthday.

The day after the birthday party the Starling, who had been away on holiday at Bournemouth, came back to Number Seventeen, Cherry Tree Lane.

'Hullo, hullo, hullo! Here we are again!' he screamed joyfully, landing with a little wobble upon the window-sill.

'Well, how's the girl?' he inquired cheekily of Mary Poppins, cocking his little head on one side and regarding her with bright, amused, twinkling eyes.

'None the better for *your* asking,' said Mary Poppins, tossing her head.

The Starling laughed.

'Same old Mary P.,' he said. 'No change out of *you*! How are the other ones – the cuckoos?' he asked, and looked across at Barbara's cot.

'Well, Barbarina,' he began in his soft, wheedling voice, 'anything for the old fellow to-day?'

'Be-lah-belah-belah-belah!' said Barbara, crooning gently as she continued to eat her arrowroot biscuit.

The Starling, with a start of surprise, hopped a little nearer.

'I said,' he repeated more distinctly, 'is there anything for the old fellow to-day, Barbie dear?'

'Ba-loo – ba-loo – ba-loo!' murmured Barbara, gazing up at the ceiling as she swallowed the last sweet crumb.

The Starling stared at her.

'Ha!' he said suddenly, and turned and looked inquiringly at Mary Poppins. Her quiet glance met his in a long look.

Then with a darting movement the Starling flew over to

John's cot and alighted on the rail. John had a large woolly lamb hugged close in his arms.

'What's my name? What's my name? What's my name?' cried the Starling in a shrill anxious voice.

'Er-umph!' said John, opening his mouth and putting the leg of the woolly lamb into it.

With a little shake of the head the Starling turned away.

'So – it's happened,' he said quietly to Mary Poppins.

She nodded.

The Starling gazed dejectedly for a moment at the Twins. Then he shrugged his speckled shoulders.

'Oh, well – I knew it would. Always told 'em so. But they wouldn't believe it.' He remained silent for a little while, staring into the cots. Then he shook himself vigorously.

'Well, well. I must be off. Back to my chimney. It will need a spring-cleaning, I'll be bound.' He flew on to the window-sill and paused, looking back over his shoulder.

'It'll seem funny without them, though. Always liked talking to them – so I did. I shall miss them.'

He brushed his wing quickly across his eyes.

'Crying?' jeered Mary Poppins. The Starling drew himself up.

'Crying? Certainly not. I have – er – a slight cold, caught on my return journey – that's all. Yes, a slight cold. Nothing serious.' He darted up to the window-pane, brushed down his breast-feathers with his beak and then, 'Cheerio!' he said perkily, and spread his wings and was gone . . .

CHAPTER 10

Full Moon

All day long Mary Poppins had been in a hurry, and when she was in a hurry she was always cross.

Everything Jane did was bad, everything Michael did was worse. She even snapped at the Twins.

Jane and Michael kept out of her way as much as possible, for they knew that there were times when it was better not to be seen or heard by Mary Poppins.

'I wish we were invisble,' said Michael, when Mary Poppins had told him that the very sight of him was more than any self-respecting person could be expected to stand.

'We shall be,' said Jane, 'if we go behind the sofa. We can count the money in our money-boxes, and she may be better after she's had her supper.'

So they did that.

'Sixpence and four pennies – that's tenpence, and a halfpenny and a threepenny-bit,' said Jane, counting up quickly.

'Four pennies and three farthings and – and that's all,' sighed Michael, putting his money in a little heap.

'That'll do nicely for the poor-box,' said Mary Poppins, looking over the arm of the sofa and sniffing.

'Oh no,' said Michael reproachfully. 'It's for myself. I'm saving.'

'Huh – for one of those aeryplanes, I suppose!' said Mary Poppins scornfully.

'No, for an elephant – a private one for myself, like Lizzie at the Zoo. I could take you for rides then,' said Michael, half-looking and half-not-looking at her to see how she would take it.

'Humph,' said Mary Poppins, 'what an idea!' But they could see she was not quite so cross as before.

'I wonder,' said Michael thoughtfully, 'what happens in the Zoo at night, when everybody's gone home?'

'Care killed a cat,' snapped Mary Poppins.

'I wasn't *caring*, I was only wondering,' corrected Michael. 'Do *you* know?' he inquired of Mary Poppins, who was whisking the crumbs off the table in double-quick time.

'One more question from you – and spit-spot, to bed you go!' she said, and began to tidy the Nursery so busily that she looked more like a whirlwind in a cap and apron than a human being.

'It's no good asking her. She knows everything, but she never tells,' said Jane.

'What's the good of knowing if you don't tell anyone?' grumbled Michael, but he said it under his breath so that Mary Poppins couldn't hear . . .

Jane and Michael could never remember having been put to bed so quickly as they were that night. Mary Poppins blew out the light very early, and went away as hurriedly as though all the winds of the world were blowing behind her.

It seemed to them that they had been there no time, however, when they heard a low voice whispering at the door.

'Hurry, Jane and Michael!' said the voice. 'Get some things on and hurry!'

They jumped out of their beds, surprised and startled.

'Come on,' said Jane. 'Something's happening.' And she began to rummage for some clothes in the darkness.

'Hurry!' called the voice again.

'Oh dear, all I can find is my sailor hat and a pair of gloves!' said Michael, running round the room pulling at drawers and feeling along shelves.

'Those'll do. Put them on. It isn't cold. Come on.'

Jane herself had only been able to find a little coat of John's, but she squeezed her arms into it and opened the door. There was nobody there, but they seemed to hear something hurrying away down the stairs. Jane and Michael followed. Whatever it was, or whoever it was, kept continually in front of them.

They never saw it, but they had the distinct sensation of being led on and on by something that constantly beckoned them to follow. Presently they were in the Lane, their slippers making a soft hissing noise on the pavement as they scurried along.

'Hurry!' urged the voice again from a near-by corner, but when they turned it they could still see nothing. They began to run, hand in hand, following the voice down streets, through alley-ways, under arches and across Parks until, panting and breathless, they were brought to a standstill beside a large turnstile in a wall.

'Here you are!' said the voice.

'Where?' called Michael to it. But there was no reply. Jane moved towards the turnstile, dragging Michael by the hand.

'Look!' she said. 'Don't you see where we are? It's the Zoo!'

A very bright full moon was shining in the sky and by its light Michael examined the iron grating and looked through the bars. Of course! How silly of him not to have known it was the Zoo!

'But how shall we get in?' he said. 'We've no money.'

'That's all right!' said a deep, gruff voice from within. 'Special Visitors allowed in free to-night. Push the wheel, please!'

Jane and Michael pushed and were through the turnstile in a second.

'Here's your ticket,' the gruff voice said, and, looking up, they found that it came from a huge Brown Bear who was wearing a coat with brass buttons and a peaked cap on his head. In his paw were two pink tickets which he held out to the children.

'But we usually *give* tickets,' said Jane.

'Usual is as usual does. To-night you receive them,' said the Bear, smiling.

Michael had been regarding him closely.

'I remember you,' he said to the Bear. 'I once gave you a tin of golden syrup.'

'You did,' said the Bear. 'And you forgot to take the lid off. Do you know, I was more than ten days working at that lid? Be more careful in the future.'

'But why aren't you in your cage? Are you always out at night?' said Michael.

'No – only when the Birthday falls on a Full Moon. But you must excuse me. I must attend to the gate.' And the Bear turned away and began to spin the handle of the turnstile again.

Jane and Michael, holding their tickets, walked on into the Zoo grounds. In the light of the full moon every tree and flower and shrub was visible, and they could see the houses and cages quite clearly.

'There seems to be a lot going on,' observed Michael.

And, indeed, there was. Animals were running about in all the paths, sometimes accompanied by birds and sometimes alone. Two wolves ran past the children, talking eagerly to a very tall stork who was tip-toeing between them with dainty, delicate movements. Jane and Michael distinctly caught the words 'Birthday' and 'Full Moon' as they went by.

In the distance three camels were strolling along side by side, and not far away a beaver and an American vulture were deep in conversation. And they all seemed to the children to be discussing the same subject.

'Whose Birthday is it, I wonder?' said Michael, but Jane was moving ahead, gazing at a curious sight.

Just by the Elephant Stand a very large, very fat old gentleman was walking up and down on all fours, and on his back, on two small parallel seats, were eight monkeys going for a ride.

'Why, it's all upside down!' exclaimed Jane.

The old gentleman gave her an angry look as he went past.

'Upside down!' he snorted. 'Me! Upside down? Certainly not. Gross insult!' The eight monkeys laughed rudely.

'Oh, please – I didn't mean you – but the whole thing,' explained Jane, hurrying after him to apologise. 'On ordinary days the animals carry human beings and now there's a human being carrying the animals. That's what I meant.'

But the old gentleman, shuffling and panting, insisted that he had been insulted, and hurried away with the monkeys screaming on his back.

Jane saw it was no good following him, so she took Michael's hand and moved onwards. They were startled when a voice, almost at their feet, hailed them.

'Come on, you two! In you come. Let's see *you* dive for a bit of orange-peel you don't want.' It was a bitter, angry voice, and looking down they saw that it came from a small black Seal who was leering at them from a moonlit pool of water.

'Come on, now – and see how *you* like it!' he said.

'But – but we can't swim!' said Michael.

'Can't help that!' said the Seal. 'You should have thought of that before. Nobody ever bothers to find out whether *I* can swim or not. Eh, what? What's that?'

He spoke the last question to another Seal who had emerged from the water and was whispering in his ear.

'Who?' said the first Seal. 'Speak up!'

The second Seal whispered again. Jane caught the words. 'Special Visitors – Friends of – ' and then no more.

The first Seal seemed disappointed, but he said politely enough to Jane and Michael:

'Oh, beg pardon. Pleased to meet you. Beg pardon.' And he held out his flipper and shook hands limply with them both.

'Look where you're going, can't you?' he shouted, as something bumped into Jane. She turned quickly and gave a little frightened start as she beheld an enormous Lion. The eyes of the Lion brightened as he saw her.

'Oh, I say –' he began. 'I didn't know it was you! This place is so crowded to-night and I'm in such a hurry to see the humans fed I'm afraid I didn't look where I was going. Coming along? You oughtn't to miss it, you know –'

'Perhaps,' said Jane politely, 'you'd show us the way.' She was a little uncertain of the Lion, but he seemed kindly enough. 'And after all,' she thought, 'everything is topsy-turvy to-night.'

'Dee-lighted!' said the Lion in rather a mincing voice, and he offered her his arm. She took it, but to be on the safe side she kept Michael beside her. He was such a round, fat little boy, and after all, she thought, lions are lions –

'Does my mane look nice?' asked the Lion as they moved off. 'I had it curled for the occasion.'

Jane looked at it. She could see that it had been carefully oiled and combed into ringlets.

'Very,' she said. 'But – isn't it rather odd for a lion to care about such things? I thought –'

'What! My dear young lady, the Lion, as you know, is the King of the Beasts. He has to remember his position.

And I, personally, am not likely to forget it. I believe a lion should *always* look his best no matter where he is. This way.'

And with a graceful wave of his forepaw he pointed towards the Big Cat House and ushered them in at the entrance.

Jane and Michael caught their breaths at the sight that met their eyes. The great hall was thronged with animals. Some were leaning over the long bar that separated them from the cages, some were standing on the seats that rose in tiers opposite. There were panthers and leopards, wolves, tigers and antelopes; monkeys and hedgehogs, wombats, mountain goats and giraffes; and an enormous group composed entirely of kittiwakes and vultures.

'Splendid, isn't it?' said the Lion proudly. 'Just like the dear old jungle days. But come along – we must get good places.'

And he pushed his way through the crowd crying, 'Gangway, gangway!' and dragging Jane and Michael after him. Presently, through a little clearing in the middle of the hall, they were able to get a glimpse of the cages.

'Why,' said Michael, opening his mouth very wide, 'they're full of human beings!'

And they were.

In one cage two large, middle-aged gentlemen in top-hats and striped trousers were prowling up and down, anxiously gazing through the bars as though they were waiting for something.

Children of all shapes and sizes, from babies in long

clothes upwards, were scrambling about in another cage. The animals outside regarded these with great interest and some of them tried to make the babies laugh by thrusting their paws or their tails in through the bars. A giraffe stretched his long neck out over the heads of the other animals and let a little boy in a sailor-suit tickle its nose.

In a third cage three elderly ladies in raincoats and goloshes were imprisoned. One of them was knitting, but the other two were standing near the bars shouting at the animals and poking at them with their umbrellas.

'Nasty brutes. Go away. I want my tea!' screamed one of them.

'Isn't she funny?' said several of the animals, and they laughed loudly at her.

'Jane – look!" said Michael, pointing to the cage at the end of the row. 'Isn't that – ?'

'Admiral Boom!' said Jane, looking very surprised.

And Admiral Boom it was. He was ramping up and down in his cage, coughing, and blowing his nose, and spluttering with rage.

'Blast my gizzard! All hands to the Pump! Land, ho! Heave away there! Blast my gizzard!' shouted the Admiral. Every time he came near the bars a tiger prodded him gently with a stick and this made Admiral Boom swear dreadfully.

'But how did they all get in there?' Jane asked the Lion.

'Lost,' said the Lion. 'Or rather, left behind. These are the people who've dawdled and been left inside when the gates were shut. Got to put 'em somewhere, so we keep

ADMIRAL
BOOM
BRITISH ISLES

'em here. He's dangerous – that one there! Nearly did for
his keeper not long ago. Don't go near him!' And he
pointed at Admiral Boom.

'Stand back, please, stand back! Don't crush! Make way,
please!' Jane and Michael could hear several voices crying
these words loudly.

'Ah – now they're going to be fed!' said the Lion, excitedly pressing forward into the crowd. 'Here come the
keepers.'

Four Brown Bears, each wearing a peaked cap, were
trundling trolleys of food along the little corridor that
separated the animals from the cages.

'Stand back, there!' they said, whenever an animal got
in the way. Then they opened a small door in each cage
and thrust the food through on pronged forks.

Jane and Michael had a good view of what was happening, through a gap between a panther and a dingo. Bottles of milk were being thrown in to the babies, who made soft little grabs with their hands and clutched them greedily. The older children snatched sponge-cakes and dough-nuts from the forks and began to eat ravenously. Plates of thin bread-and-butter and wholemeal scones were provided for the ladies in goloshes, and the gentlemen in top-hats had lamb cutlets and custard in glasses. These, as they received their food, took it away into a corner, spread handkerchiefs over their striped trousers and began to eat.

Presently, as the keepers passed down the line of cages, a great commotion was heard.

'Blast my vitals – call that a meal? A skimpy little round of beef and a couple of cabbages! What – no Yorkshire pudding? Outrageous! Up with the anchor! And where's my port? Port, I say! Heave her over! Below there, where's the Admiral's port?'

'Listen to him! He's turned nasty. I tell you, he's not safe – that one,' said the Lion.

Jane and Michael did not need to be told whom he meant. They knew Admiral Boom's. language too well.

'Well,' said the Lion, as the noise in the hall grew less uproarious. 'That appears to be the end. And I'm afraid, if you'll excuse me, I must be getting along. See you later at the Grand Chain, I hope. I'll look out for you.' And, leading them to the door, he took his leave of them, sidling away, swinging his curled mane, his golden body dappled with moonlight and shadow.

'Oh, please – ' Jane called after him. But he was out of hearing.

'I wanted to ask him if they'd ever get out. The poor humans! Why, it might have been John and Barbara – or any of us.' She turned to Michael, but found that he was no longer by her side. He had moved away along one of the paths and, running after him, she found him talking to a Penguin who was standing in the middle of the path with a large copy-book under one wing and an enormous pencil under the other. He was biting the end of it thoughtfully as she approached.

'I can't think,' she heard Michael saying, apparently in answer to a question.

The Penguin turned to Jane. 'Perhaps *you* can tell me,' he said. 'Now, what rhymes with Mary? I can't use "contrary" because that has been done before and one must be original. If you're going to say "fairy," don't. I've thought of that already, but as it's not a bit like her, it won't do.'

'Hairy,' said Michael brightly.

'H'm. Not poetic enough,' observed the Penguin.

'What about "wary"?' said Jane.

'Well – ' The Penguin appeared to be considering it. 'It's not *very* good, is it?' he said forlornly. 'I'm afraid I'll have to give it up. You see, I was trying to write a poem for the Birthday. I thought it would be so nice if I began:

'*O Mary, Mary –* '

and then I couldn't get any farther. It's very annoying. They expect something learned from a penguin, and I don't want to disappoint them. Well, well – you mustn't keep me. I must get on with it.' And with that he hurried away, biting his pencil and bending over his copy-book.

'This is all very confusing,' said Jane. 'Whose birthday is it, I wonder?'

'Now, come along, you two, come along. You want to pay your respects, I suppose, it being the Birthday and all!' said a voice behind them, and turning, they saw the Brown Bear who had given them their tickets at the gate.

'Oh, of course!' said Jane, thinking that was the safest thing to say, but not knowing in the least whom they were to pay their respects to.

The Brown Bear put an arm round each of them and propelled them along the path. They could feel his warm soft fur brushing against their bodies and hear the rumblings his voice made in his stomach as he talked.

'Here we are, *here* we are!' said the Brown Bear, stopping before a small house whose windows were all so brightly lit that if it hadn't been a moonlight night you would have thought the sun was shining. The Bear opened the door and gently pushed the two children through it.

The light dazzled them at first, but their eyes soon became accustomed to it and they saw that they were in the Snake House. All the cages were open and the snakes were out – some curled lazily into great scaly knots, others slipping gently about the floor. And in the middle of the snakes, on a log that had evidently been brought from one of the cages, sat Mary Poppins. Jane and Michael could hardly believe their eyes.

'Coupla birthday guests, ma'am,' announced the Brown

Bear respectfully. The snakes turned their heads inquiringly towards the children. Mary Poppins did not move. But she spoke.

'And where's your overcoat, may I ask?' she demanded, looking crossly but without surprise at Michael.

'And *your* hat and gloves?' she snapped, turning to Jane.

But before either of them had time to reply there was a stir in the Snake House.

'Hsssst! Hsssst!'

The snakes, with a soft hissing sound, were rising up on end and bowing to something behind Jane and Michael. The Brown Bear took off his peaked cap. And slowly Mary Poppins, too, stood up.

'My dear child. My very dear child!' said a small, delicate, hissing voice. And out from the largest of the cages there came, with slow, soft, winding movements, a Hamadryad. He slid in graceful curves past the bowing snakes and the Brown Bear, towards Mary Poppins. And when he reached her, he raised the front half of his long golden body, and, thrusting upwards his scaly golden hood, daintily kissed her, first on one cheek and then on the other.

'So!' he hissed softly. 'This is very pleasant – very pleasant, indeed. It is long since your Birthday fell on a Full Moon, my dear.' He turned his head.

'Be seated, friends!' he said, bowing graciously to the other snakes, who, at that word, slid reverently to the floor again, coiled themselves up, and gazed steadily at the Hamadryad and Mary Poppins.

The Hamadryad turned then to Jane and Michael, and

with a little shiver they saw that his face was smaller and more wizened than anything they had ever seen. They took a step forward, for his curious deep eyes seemed to draw them towards him. Long and narrow they were, with a dark sleepy look in them, and in the middle of that dark sleepiness a wakeful light like a jewel.

'And who, may I ask, are these?' he said in his soft, terrifying voice, looking at the children inquiringly.

'Miss Jane Banks and Master Michael Banks, at your service,' said the Brown Bear gruffly, as though he were half afraid. '*Her* friends.'

'Ah, *her* friends. Then they are welcome. My dears, pray be seated.'

Jane and Michael, feeling somehow that they were in the presence of a King – as they had not felt when they met the Lion – with difficulty drew their eyes from that compelling gaze and looked round for something to sit on. The Brown Bear provided this by squatting down himself and offering them each a furry knee.

Jane said, in a whisper: 'He talks as though he were a great lord.'

'He *is*. He's the lord of our world – the wisest and most terrible of us all,' said the Brown Bear softly and reverently.

The Hamadryad smiled, a long, slow, secret smile, and turned to Mary Poppins.

'Cousin,' he began, gently hissing.

'Is she *really* his cousin?' whispered Michael.

'First cousin once removed – on the mother's side,' returned the Brown Bear, whispering the information behind his paw. 'But, listen now. He's going to give the Birthday Present.'

'Cousin,' repeated the Hamadryad, 'it is long since your Birthday fell on the Full Moon and long since we have been able to celebrate the event as we celebrate it to-night. I have, therefore, had time to give the question of your Birthday Present some consideration. And I have decided' – he paused, and there was no sound in the Snake House but the sound of many creatures all holding their breath – 'that I cannot do better than give you one of my own skins.'

'Indeed, cousin, it is too kind of you –' began Mary Poppins, but the Hamadryad held up his hood for silence.

'Not at all. Not at all. You know that I change my skin from time to time and that one more or less means little to me. Am I not – ?' he paused and looked round him.

'The Lord of the Jungle,' hissed all the snakes in unison, as though the question and the answer were part of a well-known ceremony.

The Hamadryad nodded. 'So,' he said, 'what seems good to me will seem so to you. It is a small enough gift, dear Mary, but it may serve for a belt or a pair of shoes, even a hat-band – these things always come in useful, you know.'

And with that he began to sway gently from side to side, and it seemed to Jane and Michael as they watched that little waves were running up his body from the tail to the head. Suddenly he gave a long, twisting, corkscrew leap and his golden outer skin lay on the floor, and in its place he was wearing a new coat of shining silver.

'Wait!' said the Hamadryad, as Mary Poppins bent to pick up the skin. 'I will write a Greeting upon it.' And he ran his tail very quickly along his thrown skin, deftly bent the golden sheath into a circle, and diving his head through this as though it were a crown, offered it graciously to Mary Poppins. She took it, bowing.

'I just can't thank you enough – ' she began, and paused. She was evidently very pleased, for she kept running the skin backwards and forwards through her fingers and looking at it admiringly.

'Don't try,' said the Hamadryad. 'Hsst!' he went on, and spread out his hood as though he were listening with it. 'Do I not hear the signal for the Grand Chain?'

Everybody listened. A bell was ringing and a deep gruff voice could be heard coming nearer and nearer, crying out:

'Grand Chain, Grand Chain! Everybody to the centre for the Grand Chain and Finale. Come along, come along. Stand ready for the Grand Chain!'

'I thought so,' said the Hamadryad, smiling. 'You must be off, my dear. They'll be waiting for you to take your place in the centre. Farewell, till your next Birthday.' And he raised himself as he had done before and lightly saluted Mary Poppins on both cheeks.

'Hurry away!' said the Hamadryad. 'I will take care of your young friends.'

Jane and Michael felt the Brown Bear moving under them as they stood up. Past their feet they could feel all the snakes slipping and writhing as they hurried from the

Snake House. Mary Poppins bowed towards the Hamadryad very ceremoniously, and without a backward glance
at the children went running towards the huge green
square in the centre of the Zoo.

'You may leave us,' said the Hamadryad to the Brown
Bear who, after bowing humbly, ran off with his cap in
his hand to where all the other animals were congregat-
ing round Mary Poppins.

'Will you go with me?' said the Hamadryad kindly to
Jane and Michael. And without waiting for them to reply
he slid between them, and with a movement of his hood
directed them to walk one on either side of him.

'It has begun,' he said, hissing with pleasure.

And from the loud cries that were now coming from the
Green, the children could guess that he meant the Grand
Chain. As they drew nearer they could hear the animals
singing and shouting, and presently they saw leopards
and lions, beavers, camels, bears, cranes, antelopes and
many others all forming themselves into a ring round
Mary Poppins. Then the animals began to move, wildly
crying their Jungle songs, prancing in and out of the ring,
and exchanging hand and wing as they went as dancers
do in the Grand Chain of the Lancers.

A little piping voice rose high above the rest:

> '*Oh, Mary, Mary,*
> *She's my Dearie,*
> *She's my Dear-i-o!*'

And they saw the Penguin come dancing by, waving his

short wings and singing lustily. He caught sight of them, bowed to the Hamadryad, and called out:

'I got it – did you hear me singing it? It's not perfect, of course. "Dearie" does not rhyme *exactly* with Mary. But it'll do, it'll do!' and he skipped off and offered his wing to a leopard.

Jane and Michael watched the dance, the Hamadryad secret and still between them. As their friend the Lion, dancing past, bent down to take the wing of a Brazilian Pheasant in his paw, Jane shyly tried to put her feelings into words.

'I thought, Sir – ' she began and stopped, feeling confused, and not sure whether she ought to say it or not.

'Speak, my child!' said the Hamadryad. 'You thought?'

'Well – that lions and birds, and tigers and little animals – '

The Hamadryad helped her. 'You thought that they were natural enemies, that the lion could not meet a bird without eating it, nor the tiger the hare – eh?'

Jane blushed and nodded.

'Ah – you may be right. It is probable. But not on the Birthday,' said the Hamadryad. 'To-night the small are free from the great and the great protect the small. Even I – ' he paused and seemed to be thinking deeply, 'even *I* can meet a Barnacle Goose without any thought of dinner – on this occasion. And after all,' he went on, flicking his terrible little forked tongue in and out as he spoke, 'it may be that to eat and be eaten are the same thing in the end. My wisdom tells me that this is probably so. We are all made of the same stuff, remember, we of the

Forming themselves into a ring round Mary Poppins

Jungle, you of the City. The same substance composes us –
the tree overhead, the stone beneath us, the bird, the beast,
the star – we are all one, all moving to the same end.
Remember that when you no longer remember me, my
child.'

'But how can tree be stone? A bird is not me. Jane is not
a tiger,' said Michael stoutly.

'You think not?' said the Hamadryad's hissing voice.
'Look!' and he nodded his head towards the moving mass
of creatures before them. Birds and animals were now
swaying together, closely encircling Mary Poppins, who
was rocking lightly from side to side. Backwards and for-

wards went the swaying crowd, keeping time together, swinging like the pendulum of a clock. Even the trees were bending and lifting gently, and the moon seemed to be rocking in the sky as a ship rocks on the sea.

'Bird and beast and stone and star – we are all one, all one – ' murmured the Hamadryad, softly folding his hood about him as he himself swayed between the children.

'Child and serpent, star and stone – all one.'

The hissing voice grew softer. The cries of the swaying animals dwindled and became faster. Jane and Michael, as they listened, felt themselves gently rocking too, or as if they were being rocked . . .

Soft, shaded light fell on their faces.

'Asleep and dreaming – both of them,' said a whispering voice. Was it the voice of the Hamadryad, or their Mother's voice as she tucked them in, on her usual nightly round of the Nursery?

'Good.' Was that the Brown Bear gruffly speaking, or Mr Banks?

Jane and Michael, rocking and swaying, could not tell . . . could not tell . . .

'I had such a strange dream last night,' said Jane, as she sprinkled sugar over her porridge at breakfast. 'I dreamed we were at the Zoo and it was Mary Poppins' birthday, and instead of animals in the cages there were human beings, and all the animals were outside – '

'Why, that's *my* dream. *I* dreamed that, too,' said Michael, looking very surprised.

'We can't both have dreamed the same thing,' said Jane.
'Are you sure? Do you remember the Lion who curled his
mane and the Seal who wanted us to –'

'Dive for orange-peel?' said Michael. 'Of course I do!
And the babies inside the cage, and the Penguin who
couldn't find a rhyme, and the Hamadryad –'

'Then it couldn't have been a dream at all,' said Jane
emphatically. 'It must have been *true*. And if it was –' She
looked curiously at Mary Poppins, who was boiling the
milk.

'Mary Poppins,' she said, 'could Michael and I have
dreamed the same dream?'

'You and your dreams!' said Mary Poppins, sniffing.
'Eat your porridge, please, or you will have no buttered
toast.'

But Jane would not be put off. She *had* to know.

'Mary Poppins,' she said, looking very hard at her,
'were you at the Zoo last night?'

Mary Poppins' eyes popped.

'At the Zoo? In the middle of the night? Me? A quiet
orderly person who knows that early to bed, early to rise
makes a man healthy, wealthy and wise?'

'But *were* you?' Jane persisted.

'I have all I need of Zoos in this nursery, thank you,'
said Mary Poppins, uppishly. 'Hyenas, ourang-outangs, all
of you. Sit up straight, and no more nonsense.'

Jane poured out her milk.

'Then it must have been a dream,' she said, 'after all.'

But Michael was staring, open-mouthed, at Mary
Poppins, who was now making toast at the fire.

'Jane,' he said in a shrill whisper, 'Jane, look!' He pointed, and Jane, too, saw what he was looking at.

Round her waist Mary Poppins was wearing a belt made of golden scaly snake-skin, and on it was written in curving, snaky writing:

A PRESENT FROM THE ZOO.

CHAPTER II

Christmas Shopping

'I smell snow,' said Jane, as they got out of the Bus.

'I smell Christmas trees,' said Michael.

'I smell fried fish,' said Mary Poppins.

And then there was no time to smell anything else, for the Bus had stopped outside the Largest Shop in the World, and they were all going into it to do their Christmas shopping.

'May we look at the windows first?' said Michael, hopping excitedly on one leg.

'I don't mind,' said Mary Poppins with surprising mildness. Not that Jane and Michael were *really* very surprised, for they knew that the thing Mary Poppins liked doing best of all was looking in shop windows. They knew, too, that while they saw toys and books and holly-boughs and plum cakes, Mary Poppins saw nothing but herself reflected there.

'Look, aeroplanes!' said Michael, as they stopped before a window in which toy aeroplanes were careering through the air on wires.

'And look there!' said Jane. 'Two tiny black babies in one cradle – are they chocolate, do you think, or china?'

'Just look at *you!*' said Mary Poppins to herself, particularly noticing how nice her new gloves with the fur tops looked. They were the first pair she had ever had, and she thought she would never grow tired of looking at them in the shop windows with her hands inside them. And having examined the reflection of the gloves she went carefully over her whole person – coat, hat, scarf and shoes, with herself inside – and she thought that, on the

whole, she had never seen anybody looking quite so smart and distinguished.

But the winter afternoons, she knew, were short, and they had to be home by tea-time. So with a sigh she wrenched herself away from her glorious reflection.

'Now we will go in,' she said, and annoyed Jane and Michael very much by lingering at the Haberdashery counter and taking great trouble over the choice of a reel of black cotton.

'The Toy Department,' Michael reminded her, 'is in *that* direction.'

'I know, thank you. Don't point,' she said, and paid her bill with aggravating slowness.

But at last they found themselves alongside Father Christmas, who went to the greatest trouble in helping them choose their presents.

'That will do nicely for Daddy,' said Michael, selecting a clockwork train with special signals. 'I will take care of it for him when he goes to the City.'

'I think I will get this for Mother,' said Jane, pushing a small doll's perambulator which, she felt sure, her Mother had always wanted. 'Perhaps she will lend it to me sometimes.'

After that, Michael chose a packet of hairpins for each of the Twins and a Meccano set for his Mother, a mechanical beetle for Robertson Ay, a pair of spectacles for Ellen, whose eyesight was perfectly good, and some bootlaces for Mrs Brill who always wore slippers.

Jane, after some hesitation, eventually decided that a white dickey would be just the thing for Mr Banks, and she bought *Robinson Crusoe* for the Twins to read when they grew up.

'Until they are old enough, I can read it myself,' she said. 'I am sure they will lend it to me.'

Mary Poppins then had a great argument with Father Christmas over a cake of soap.

'Why not Lifebuoy?' said Father Christmas, trying to be

helpful and looking anxiously at Mary Poppins, for she was being rather snappy.

'I prefer Vinolia,' she said haughtily, and she bought a cake of that.

'My goodness,' she said, smoothing the fur on her right-hand glove. 'I wouldn't half like a cup of tea!'

'Would you quarter like it, though?' asked Michael.

'There is no call for you to be funny,' said Mary Poppins, in such a voice that Michael felt that, indeed, there wasn't.

'And it is time to go home.'

There! She had said the very words they had been hoping she wouldn't say. That was so like Mary Poppins.

'Just five minutes longer,' pleaded Jane.

'Ah do, Mary Poppins! You look so nice in your new gloves,' said Michael wilily.

But Mary Poppins, though she appreciated the remark, was not taken in by it.

'No,' she said, and closed her mouth with a snap and stalked towards the doorway.

'Oh, dear!' said Michael to himself, as he followed her, staggering under the weight of his parcels. 'If only she would say "Yes" for once!'

But Mary Poppins hurried on and they had to go with her. Behind them Father Christmas was waving his hand, and the Fairy Queen on the Christmas tree and all the other dolls were smiling sadly and saying, 'Take me home, somebody!' and the aeroplanes were all beating their wings and saying in bird-like voices, 'Let me fly! Ah, do let me fly!'

Jane and Michael hurried away, closing their ears to those enchanting voices, and feeling that the time in the Toy Department had been unreasonably and cruelly short.

And then, just as they came towards the shop entrance, the adventure happened.

They were just about to spin the glass door and go out, when they saw coming towards it from the pavement the running, flickering figure of a child.

'Look!' said Jane and Michael both together.

'My gracious, goodness, glory me!' exclaimed Mary Poppins, and stood still.

And well she might, for the child had practically no clothes on, only a light wispy strip of blue stuff that looked as though she had torn it from the sky to wrap round her naked body.

It was evident that she did not know much about spinning doors, for she went round and round inside it, pushing it so that it should spin faster and laughing as it caught her and sent her whirling round and round. Then suddenly, with a quick little movement she freed herself, sprang away from it and landed inside the shop.

She paused on tip-toe, turning her head this way and that, as though she were looking for someone. Then, with a start of pleasure, she caught sight of Jane and Michael and Mary Poppins as they stood, half-hidden behind an enormous fir-tree, and ran towards them joyously.

'Ah, *there* you are! Thank you for waiting. I'm afraid I'm a little late,' said the child, stretching out her bright arms to Jane and Michael. 'Now,' she cocked her head on one side, 'aren't you glad to see me? Say yes, say yes!'

'Yes,' said Jane smiling, for nobody, she felt, could help being glad to see anyone so bright and happy. 'But who are you?' she inquired curiously.

'What is your name?' said Michael, gazing at her.

'Who am I? What is my name? Don't say you don't know me? Oh, surely, surely – ' The child seemed very surprised and a little disappointed. She turned suddenly to Mary Poppins and pointed her finger.

'*She* knows me. Don't you? I'm sure you know me!'

There was a curious look on Mary Poppins' face. Jane and Michael could see blue fires in her eyes as though they reflected the blue of the child's dress and her brightness.

'Does it – does it,' she whispered, 'begin with an M?'

The child hopped on one leg delightedly.

'Of course it does – and you know it. M-A-I-A. I'm Maia.' She turned to Jane and Michael.

'*Now* you recognise me, don't you? I'm the second of the Pleiades. Electra – she's the eldest – couldn't come because she's minding Merope. Merope's the baby, and the other five of us come in between – all girls. Our Mother was very disappointed at first not to have a boy, but now she doesn't mind.'

The child danced a few steps and burst out again in her excited little voice:

'Oh, Jane! Oh, Michael – I've often watched you from the sky, and now I'm actually talking to you. There is nothing about you I don't know. Michael doesn't like having his hair brushed, and Jane has a thrush's egg in a jam-jar on the mantelpiece. And your Father is going bald on the top. I like him. It was he who first introduced us – don't you remember? He said one evening last summer:

' "Look, there are the Pleiades. Seven stars all together, the smallest in the sky. But there is one of them you can't see."

'He meant Merope, of course. She's still too young to stay up all night. She's such a baby that she has to go to bed very early. Some of them up there call us the Little Sisters, and sometimes we are called the Seven Doves, but Orion calls us "You girls" and takes us hunting with him.'

'But what are you doing here?' demanded Michael, still very surprised.

Maia laughed. 'Ask Mary Poppins. I am sure she knows.'

'Tell us, Mary Poppins,' said Jane.

'Well,' said Mary Poppins snappily, 'I suppose you two aren't the only ones in the world that want to go shopping at Christmas – '

'That's it,' squealed Maia delightedly. 'She's quite right. I've come down to buy toys for them all. We can't get away very often, you know, because we're so busy making and storing up the Spring Rains. That's the special job of the Pleiades. However, we drew lots and I won. Wasn't it lucky?'

She hugged herself happily.

'Now, come on. I can't stay very long. And you must come back and help me choose.'

And dancing about them, running now to one and now to another, she shepherded them back to the Toy Department. As they went, the crowds of shoppers stood and stared at them and dropped their parcels with astonishment.

'So cold for her. What can her parents be thinking of!' said the Mothers, with voices that were suddenly soft and gentle.

'I mean to say – !' said the Fathers. 'It shouldn't be allowed. Must write to *The Times* about it.' And their voices were unnaturally gruff and gritty.

The shop-walkers behaved curiously, too. As the little group passed they bowed to Maia as though she were a Queen.

But none of them – not Jane, nor Michael, nor Mary Poppins, nor Maia – noticed nor heard anything extraordinary. They were too busy with their own extraordinary adventure.

'Here we are!' said Maia, as she pranced into the Toy Department. 'Now, what shall we choose?'

An Assistant, with a start, bowed respectfully as soon as he saw her.

'I want something for each of my sisters – six of them. You must help me, please,' said Maia, smiling at him.

'Certainly, madam,' said the Assistant agreeably.

'First – my eldest sister,' said Maia. 'She's very domestic. What about that little stove with the silver saucepans? Yes. And that striped broom. We are so troubled with star-dust, and she will love having that to sweep it up with.'

The Assistant began wrapping the things in coloured paper.

'Now for Taygete. She likes dancing. Don't you think, Jane, a skipping-rope would be just the thing for her? You'll tie them carefully, won't you?' she said to the Assistant. 'I have a long way to go.'

She fluttered on among the toys, never standing still for a moment, but walking with a light quicksilver step, as though she were still twinkling in the sky.

Mary Poppins and Jane and Michael could not take their eyes off her as she flickered from one of them to another asking their advice.

'Then there's Alcyone. She's difficult. She's so quiet and thoughtful and never seems to want anything. A book, do you think, Mary Poppins? What is this Family – the *Swiss-Robinsons*? I think she would like that. And if she doesn't, she can look at the pictures. Wrap it up!'

She handed the book to the Assistant.

'I know what Celæno wants,' she went on. 'A hoop. She can bowl it across the sky in the day-time and make a circle of it to spin about her at night. She'll love that red and blue one.' The Assistant bowed again and began to wrap up the hoop.

'Now there are only the two little ones left. Michael, what would you advise for Sterope?'

'What about a top?' said Michael, giving the question his earnest consideration.

'A humming-top? *What* a good idea! She will love to watch it go waltzing and singing down the sky. And what do you think for Merope, the baby, Jane?'

'John and Barbara,' said Jane shyly, 'have rubber ducks!'

Maia gave a delighted squeal and hugged herself.

'Oh, Jane, how wise you are! I should never have thought of that. A rubber duck for Merope, please – a blue one with yellow eyes.'

The Assistant tied up the parcels, while Maia ran round him, pushing at the paper, giving a tug to the string to make sure that it was firmly knotted.

'That's right,' she said. 'You see, I mustn't drop anything.'

Michael, who had been staring steadily at her ever since she first appeared, turned and said in a loud whisper to Mary Poppins:

'But she has no purse. Who will pay for the toys?'

'None of your business,' snapped Mary Poppins.

'And it's rude to whisper.' But she began to fumble busily in her pocket.

'What did you say?' demanded Maia with round, surprised eyes. 'Pay? Nobody will pay. There is nothing to pay – is there?'

She turned her shining gaze upon the Assistant.

'Nothing at all, madam,' he assured her, as he put the parcels into her arms and bowed again.

'I thought not. You see,' she said, turning to Michael, 'the whole point of Christmas is that things should be *given* away, isn't it? Besides, what could I pay with? We have no money up there.' And she laughed at the mere suggestion of such a thing.

'Now we must go,' she went on, taking Michael's arm. 'We must all go home. It's very late, and I heard your Mother telling you that you must be home in time for tea. Besides, I must get back, too. Come.' And drawing Michael and Jane and Mary Poppins after her, she led the way through the shop and out by the spinning door.

Outside the entrance Jane suddenly said:

'But there's no present for *her*. She's bought something for all the others and nothing for herself. Maia has no Christmas present.' And she began to search hurriedly through the parcels she was carrying, to see what she could spare for Maia.

Mary Poppins gave a quick glance into the window beside her. She saw herself shining back at her, very smart, very interesting, her hat on straight, her coat nicely pressed and her new gloves just completing the whole effect.

'You be quiet,' she said to Jane in her snappiest voice. At the same time she whipped off her new gloves and thrust one on to each of Maia's hands.

'There!' she said gruffly. 'It's cold to-day. You'll be glad of them.'

Maia looked at the gloves, hanging very large and almost empty upon her hands. She said nothing, but moving close to Mary Poppins she reached up her spare arm and put it round Mary Poppins' neck and kissed her. A long look passed between them, and they smiled as people smile who understand each other. Maia turned then, and with her hand lightly touched the cheeks of Jane and Michael. And for a moment they all stood in a ring at the windy corner gazing at each other as though they were enchanted.

'I've been so happy,' said Maia softly, breaking the silence. 'Don't forget me, will you?'

They shook their heads.

'Good-bye,' said Maia.

'Good-bye,' said the others, though it was the last thing they wanted to say.

Then Maia, standing poised on tip-toe, lifted up her arms and sprang into the air. She began to step, climbing ever higher, as though there were invisible stairs cut into the grey sky. She waved to them as she went, and the three of them waved back.

'What on earth is happening?' somebody said close by.

'But it's not possible!' said another voice.

'Preposterous!' cried a third. For a crowd was gathering to witness the extraordinary sight of Maia returning home.

A Policeman pushed his way through the throng, scattering the people with his truncheon.

"'Ere! Come down! We can't 'ave this kind of thing!"

'Naow, naow. Wot's all this? A Naccident or wot?'

He looked up, his gaze following that of the rest of the crowd.

''Ere!' he called angrily, shaking his fist at Maia. 'Come down! Wot you doing up there? 'Olding up the traffic and all. Come down! We can't 'ave this kind of thing – not in a public place. 'Tisn't natural!'

Far away they heard Maia laughing and saw something bright dangling from her arm. It was the skipping-rope. After all, the parcel had come undone.

For a moment longer they saw her prancing up the airy stair, and then a bank of cloud hid her from their eyes. They knew she was behind it, though, because of the brightness that shone about its thick dark edge.

'Well, I'm jiggered!' said the Policeman, staring upwards, and scratching his head under its helmet.

'And well you might be!' said Mary Poppins, with such a ferocious snap that anyone else might have thought she was really cross with the Policeman. But Jane and Michael were not taken in by that snap. For they could see in Mary Poppins' eyes something that, if she were anybody else but Mary Poppins, might have been described as tears . . .

'Could we have imagined it?' said Michael, when they got home and told the story to their Mother.

'Perhaps,' said Mrs Banks. 'We imagine strange and lovely things, my darling.'

'But what about Mary Poppins' gloves?' said Jane. 'We saw her give them away to Maia. And she's not wearing them now. So it must be true!'

'What, Mary Poppins!' exclaimed Mrs Banks. 'Your best fur-topped gloves! You gave them away!'

Mary Poppins sniffed.

'My gloves are my gloves and I do what I like with them!' she said haughtily.

And she straightened her hat and went down to the kitchen to have her tea . . .

CHAPTER 12

West Wind

It was the first day of Spring.

Jane and Michael knew this at once, because they heard Mr Banks singing in his bath, and there was only one day in the year when he did that.

They always remembered that particular morning. For one thing, it was the first time they were allowed to come downstairs for breakfast, and for another Mr Banks lost his black bag. So that the day began with two extra-ordinary happenings.

'Where is my *BAG*?' shouted Mr Banks, turning round and round in the hall like a dog chasing its tail.

And everybody else began running round and round too – Ellen and Mrs Brill and the children. Even Robert-son Ay made a special effort and turned round twice. At last Mr Banks discovered the bag himself in his study, and he rushed into the hall with it, holding it aloft.

'Now,' he said, as though he were delivering a sermon, 'my bag is always kept in one place. Here. On the umbrella-stand. Who put it in the study?' he roared.

'You did, my dear, when you took the Income Tax papers out of it last night,' said Mrs Banks.

Mr Banks gave her such a hurt look that she wished she had been less tactless and had said she had put it there herself.

'Humph – Urrumph!' he said, blowing his nose very hard and taking his overcoat from its peg. He walked with it to the front door.

'Hullo,' he said more cheerfully, 'the Parrot Tulips are in bud!' He went into the garden and sniffed the air. 'H'm, wind's in the West, I think.' He looked down towards Admiral Boom's house where the telescope weathercock swung. 'I thought so,' he said. 'Westerly weather. Bright and balmy. I won't take an overcoat.'

And with that he picked up his bag and his bowler hat and hurried away to the City.

'Did you hear what he said?' Michael grabbed Jane's arm.

She nodded. 'The wind's in the West,' she said slowly.

Neither of them said any more, but there was a thought in each of their minds that they wished was not there.

They forgot it soon, however, for everything seemed to be as it always was, and the Spring sunlight lit up the house so beautifully that nobody remembered it needed a coat of paint and new wallpapers. On the contrary, they all found themselves thinking that it was the best house in Cherry Tree Lane.

But trouble began after luncheon.

Jane had gone down to dig in the garden with Robertson Ay. She had just sown a row of radish-seed when she heard a great commotion in the Nursery and the sound of hurrying footsteps on the stairs. Presently Michael appeared, very red in the face and panting loudly.

'Look, Jane, look!' he cried, and held out his hand.

Within it lay Mary Poppins' compass, with the disc frantic-
ally swinging round the arrow as it trembled in Michael's
shaking hand.

'The compass?' said Jane, and looked at him question-
ingly.

Michael suddenly burst into tears.

'She gave it to me,' he wept. 'She said I could have it all
for myself now. Oh, oh, there must be something wrong!
What is going to happen? She has never given me anything
before.'

'Perhaps she was only being nice,' said Jane to soothe
him, but in her heart she felt as disturbed as Michael was.
She knew very well that Mary Poppins never wasted time
in being nice.

And yet, strange to say, during that afternoon Mary
Poppins never said a cross word. Indeed, she hardly said a
word at all. She seemed to be thinking very deeply, and
when they asked questions she answered them in a far-
away voice. At last Michael could bear it no longer.

'Oh, do be cross, Mary Poppins! Do be cross again! It is
not like you. Oh, I feel so anxious.' And indeed, his heart
felt heavy with the thought that something, he did not
quite know what, was about to happen at Number Seventeen, Cherry Tree Lane.

'Trouble trouble and it will trouble you!' retorted Mary
Poppins crossly, in her usual voice.

And immediately he felt a little better.

'Perhaps it's only a feeling,' he said to Jane. 'Perhaps
everything is all right and I'm just imagining – don't you
think so, Jane?'

'Probably,' said Jane slowly. But she was thinking hard and her heart felt tight in her body.

The wind grew wilder towards evening, and blew in little gusts about the house. It went pulling and whistling down the chimneys, slipping in through the cracks under the windows, turning the Nursery carpet up at the corners.

Mary Poppins gave them their supper and cleared away the things, stacking them neatly and methodically. Then she tidied up the Nursery and put the kettle on the hob.

'There!' she said, glancing round the room to see that everything was all right. She was silent for a minute. Then she put one hand lightly on Michael's head and the other on Jane's shoulder.

'Now,' she said, 'I am just going to take the shoes down for Robertson Ay to clean. Behave yourselves, please, till I come back.' She went out and shut the door quietly behind her.

Suddenly, as she went, they both felt they must run after her, but something seemed to stop them. They remained quiet, with their elbows on the table waiting for her to come back. Each was trying to reassure the other without saying anything.

'How silly we are,' said Jane presently. 'Everything's all right.' But she knew she said it more to comfort Michael than because she thought it was true.

The Nursery clock ticked loudly from the mantelpiece. The fire flickered and crackled and slowly died down. They still sat there at the table, waiting.

At last Michael said uneasily: 'She's been gone a very ong time, hasn't she?'

The wind whistled and cried about the house as if n reply. The clock went on ticking its solemn double note.

Suddenly the silence was broken by the sound of the ront door shutting with a loud bang.

'Michael!' said Jane, starting up.

'Jane!' said Michael, with a white, anxious look on his ace.

They listened. Then they ran quickly to the window nd looked out.

Down below, just outside the front door, stood Mary oppins, dressed in her coat and hat, with her carpet-bag n one hand and her umbrella in the other. The wind was lowing wildly about her, tugging at her skirt, tilting her at rakishly to one side. But it seemed to Jane and Michael hat she did not mind, for she smiled as though she and he wind understood each other.

She paused for a moment on the step and glanced back owards the front door. Then with a quick movement she pened the umbrella, though it was not raining, and nrust it over her head.

The wind, with a wild cry, slipped under the umbrella, ressing it upwards as though trying to force it out of lary Poppins' hand. But she held on tightly, and that, pparently, was what the wind wanted her to do, for resently it lifted the umbrella higher into the air and lary Poppins from the ground. It carried her lightly so hat her toes just grazed along the garden path. Then it

lifted her over the front gate and swept her upwards
towards the branches of the cherry trees in the Lane.

'She's going, Jane, she's going!' cried Michael, weeping.

'Quick!' cried Jane. 'Let us get the Twins. They must see
the last of her.' She had no doubt now, nor had Michael,
that Mary Poppins had gone for good because the wind
had changed.

They each seized a Twin and rushed back to the window.

Mary Poppins was in the upper air now, floating away

Floating away over the roofs of the houses

over the cherry trees and the roofs of the houses, holding tightly to the umbrella with one hand and to the carpet-bag with the other.

The Twins began to cry quietly.

With their free hands Jane and Michael opened the window and made one last effort to stay Mary Poppins' flight.

'Mary Poppins!' they cried. 'Mary Poppins, come back!'

But she either did not hear or deliberately took no notice. For she went sailing on and on, up into the cloudy, whistling air, till at last she was wafted away over the hill and the children could see nothing but the trees bending and moaning under the wild west wind . . .

'She did what she said she would, anyway. She stayed till the wind changed,' said Jane, sighing and turning sadly from the window. She took John to his cot and put him into it. Michael said nothing, but as he brought Barbara back and tucked her into bed he was sniffing uncomfortably.

'I wonder,' said Jane, 'if we'll ever see her again?'

Suddenly they heard voices on the stairs.

'Children, children!' Mrs Banks was calling as she opened the door. 'Children – I am very cross. Mary Poppins has left us – '

'Yes,' said Jane and Michael.

'You knew, then?' said Mrs Banks, rather surprised. 'Did she tell you she was going?'

They shook their heads, and Mrs Banks went on:

'It's outrageous. One minute here and gone the next. Not even an apology. Simply said, "I'm going!" and off she

ent. Anything more preposterous, more thoughtless,
ore discourteous – What is it, Michael?' She broke off
ossly, for Michael had grasped her skirt in his hands and
as shaking her. 'What *is* it, child?'

'Did she say she'd come back?' he cried, nearly knocking
s Mother over. 'Tell me – did she?'

'You will *not* behave like a Red Indian, Michael,' she said,
osening his hold. 'I don't remember *what* she said, except
at she was going. But I certainly shan't have her back if
e does want to come. Leaving me high and dry with
body to help me and without a word of notice.'

'Oh, Mother!' said Jane reproachfully.

'You are a very cruel woman,' said Michael, clenching
s fist, as though at any minute he would have to strike
er.

'Children! I'm ashamed of you – really I am! To want
ck anybody who has treated your Mother so badly. I'm
terly shocked.'

Jane burst into tears.

'Mary Poppins is the only person I want in the world!'
ichael wailed, and flung himself on to the floor.

'Really, children, really! I don't understand you. Do be
od, I beg of you. There's nobody to look after you to-
ght. I have to go out to dinner and it's Ellen's Day Off.
shall have to send Mrs Brill up.' And she kissed them
sentmindedly, and went away with an anxious little
e on her forehead . . .

Vell, if I ever did! Her going away and leaving you pore

dear children in the lurch like that,' said Mrs Brill,
moment later, bustling in and setting to work on them

'A heart of stone, that's what that girl had *and* no mi
take, or my name's not Clara Brill. Always keeping he
self to herself, too, and not even a lace handkerchief or
hatpin to remember her by. Get up, will you please, Maste
Michael!' Mrs Brill went on, panting heavily.

'How we stood her so long, I *don't* know – with her ai
and graces and all. What a lot of buttons, Miss Jan
Stand still do now, and let me undress you, Maste
Michael. Plain she was, too, nothing much to look a
Indeed, all things considered, I don't know that we won
be better off, after all. Now, Miss Jane, where's your nigh
gown – why, what's this under your pillow – ?'

Mrs Brill had drawn out a small nobbly parcel.

'What is it? Give it to me – give it,' said Jane, tremblin
with excitement, and she took it from Mrs Brill's hand
very quickly. Michael came and stood near her an
watched her undo the string and tear away the brow
paper. Mrs Brill, without waiting to see what emerge
from the package, went in to the Twins.

The last wrapping fell to the floor and the thing tha
was in the parcel lay in Jane's hand.

'It's her picture,' she said in a whisper, looking closely a
it.

And it was!

Inside a little curly frame was a painting of Mary Po
pins, and underneath it was written, 'Mary Poppins b
Bert.'

'That's the Match Man – he did it,' said Michael, and took it in his hand so that he could have a better look.

Jane found suddenly that there was a letter attached to the painting. She unfolded it carefully. It ran:

'Dear Jane,
   Michael had the compass so the picture is for you. Au revoir.

                                        MARY POPPINS'

She read it out loud till she came to the words she couldn't understand.

'Mrs Brill!' she called. 'What does "au revoir" mean?'

'Au revore, dearie?' shrieked Mrs Brill from the next room. 'Why, doesn't it mean – let me see, I'm not up in these foreign tongues – doesn't it mean "God bless you"? No. No, I'm wrong. I think, Miss Jane dear, it means "To Meet Again".'

Jane and Michael looked at each other. Joy and understanding shone in their eyes. They knew what Mary Poppins meant.

Michael gave a long sigh of relief. 'That's all right,' he said shakily. 'She always does what she says she will.' He turned away.

'Michael, are you crying?' Jane asked.

He twisted his head and tried to smile at her.

'No, I am not,' he said. 'It is only my eyes.'

She pushed him gently towards his bed, and as he got in she slipped the portrait of Mary Poppins into his hand – hurriedly, in case she should regret it.

'You have it for to-night, darling,' whispered Jane, and she tucked him in just as Mary Poppins used to do . . .

The Donkey Rustlers

GERALD DURRELL

This lively story with a Greek island setting tells how
Amanda and David plot to outwit the unpleasant local
mayor and help their Greek friend, Yani. The villagers,
and especially the mayor, depend on their donkeys for
transport. If the children are to blackmail them successfully
the donkeys must disappear – and disappear they do, to
the consternation of the whole village . . .

Told in Gerald Durrell's dashing style with his own
particular brand of humour, this story will be eagerly read
by older children.

Caldicott Place

NOEL STREATFEILD

If your father had been very badly hurt in a car crash
and then an old lady suddenly left you an enormous
rambling house in the country, would you be pleased
or not? Tim thought it was splendid: he was sure living
outside London would help his father get better. But
Tim did not have to worry about where the money was
coming from to feed and clothe him and his brother
and sister. So his mother decided to take in paying guests
– three children who had plenty of money but no real
home.

Noel Streatfeild's delightful story tells how the six
children gradually make friends; how the enormous
shabby house becomes a home to them all; and how
Tim's father gradually begins to get better. It will appeal
to everyone of eight and over.

Dolphin Boy

MARGARET MACKAY

Wiki, the young dolphin, is a lonely orphan. She has lost
her mother to a killer whale. So now she swims alone
through the waters of Calabash Cove, with only the
fishing boats to keep her company. But when she saves
Kamuelo from drowning, the Hawaiian boy and the dolphin
become firm friends.

Soon all the children from the Cove play happily with
Wiki. She clowns and dances and whistles for them, but
Kamuelo remains her favourite. They spend hours together,
Kamuelo riding on her back through the waves.

But one day Wiki's life is endangered by a giant tidal
wave. Kamuelo and his friends must struggle desperately
to save her. . . .

The Sword in the Stone

T. H. WHITE

Probably only the magician, Merlyn, knew that his pupil the Wart (to rhyme with 'Art') would one day be the great King Arthur.

For six years Merlyn was the boy's tutor and the Wart learned all manner of useful things; such as what it is like to be a fish or a hawk or a badger.

Then the king, Pendragon, died without heirs. And King Pellinore arrived at the court with an extraordinary story of a sword stuck in an anvil stuck to a stone outside a church in London. Written on the sword in gold letters were the words

Whoso Pulleth Out This Sword of
This Stone and Anvil, is Rightwise
King Born of All England.

The last person anybody expected to pull out the sword was the Wart but then he had had Merlyn as his tutor for the past six years.